Robert Sanderson

Frae the Lyne Valley

Poems and Sketches

Robert Sanderson

Frae the Lyne Valley
Poems and Sketches

ISBN/EAN: 9783744765589

Printed in Europe, USA, Canada, Australia, Japan

Cover: Foto ©Andreas Hilbeck / pixelio.de

More available books at **www.hansebooks.com**

POEMS AND SKETCHES

BY

ROBERT SANDERSON,

WEST LINTON, PEEBLESSHIRE.

———

J. AND R. PARLANE, PAISLEY.

J. MENZIES AND CO., EDINBURGH AND GLASGOW.

1888.

THIS LITTLE VOLUME

IS GRATEFULLY, AFFECTIONATELY, AND RESPECTFULLY

DEDICATED

To the Memory of Devoted and Kind Parents,

WHO

IN THEIR DAY AND GENERATION
SOUGHT ASSIDUOUSLY TO FULFIL THE DUTIES OF THEIR STATION,

AND

WERE UNWEARIED IN THEIR EFFORTS TO BESTOW UPON THEIR FAMILY
AN EDUCATION AND A TRAINING BEFITTING THEIR NECESSITIES
IN SEEKING TO FIGHT FAITHFULLY
THE BATTLE OF LIFE,

PREFACE.

In bringing this little volume to the light, the writer has little apology to offer, further than that owing to having published a lesser work fully twenty years ago, he has often felt the truth of the opinion of some of his reviewers at that period, that he had gone before the world with his wares at a time of life which might be regarded as premature. For many years back he has desired to publish in a collective form a selection from the pieces composed from time to time within the last twenty years. In this he has been encouraged by many friends both at home and abroad; but while hopeful it may contribute to the enjoyment of such, he has no desire to avoid the fair and honest criticism of the press.

Had this work appeared two years ago, the writer would in its preparation have been assisted by his esteemed and intimate friend James Smith, whose lamented death took place last year. He has, however, been assisted by other friends whose services he values very highly ; and to them and to all interested, he tenders his sincere thanks, cherishing as he does the hope that the collection as a whole will justify the lively interest they have taken in it.

R. S.

West Linton,
4th August, 1888.

CONTENTS

6 CONTENTS.

CONTENTS.   7

POEMS,

MUSINGS BY THE LYNE WATER.

Occasioned by the receipt of a kind letter from an old schoolmate, now in Ontario, to whom these verses are respectfully dedicated. 1880.

Now that the dreary drenching rains
    Their latest vials have outpoured,
And when the wide-spread fruitful plains
    To summer beauty are restored,

My favourite haunts I seek anew
    Where wind the waters of the Lyne;
Scenes that bring vividly to view
    The sunny days o' Auld Langsyne.

Here, then, amid this peaceful scene
    Of foliage rich and flowers profuse,
Let me attempt to seek again
    The favours of the lowly muse.

Here where I oft have revell'd long
    Amongst the bards in life's young day,
When balmy evenings found me 'mong
    The scenery which I now survey,

With Ramsay, Burns, or Tannahill;
    With Milton, Wordsworth, Young, or Graham;
Here o'er their page I'll ponder still,
    And seek to kindle at their flame.

B

Not to the lordly or the great,
  Or those whom men may term the same,
My homespun lays I dedicate—
  Let lowlier ones my friendship claim.

But unto one who loved to tread
  These broomy braes, that shady dell,
Who toils and sweats for honest bread,
  And fights life's battle brave and well.

A plain and honest type withal
  Of those who shall in future be
The great, the influential,
  The genuine nobility.

Yes! for the sun of idle names
  And silly titles soon shall set ;
And only they who win them shall
  Wear star, or wreath, or coronet.

Here where I frame my humble hymn,
  Here where I wake my lowly lays,
I seat me 'mong the yellow broom,
  The bonny broom on Leadlaw's braes.

While from the dense, deep, woody maze
  Embosoming the streamlet clear,
Lyne's waters, murmuring, gently raise
  Their ceaseless song to soothe the ear.

And in the distance tower the hills,
  Whose heathy sides we oft did climb ;
The nursing place of prattling rills,
  And many a pure pellucid stream.

While in the deeper vale below
  The tapering spires that heavenward rise
Tell where, half-hidden from the view,
  The quaint and ancient hamlet lies.

The landscape now before me spread
  With lake and tower and spreading tree ;
With light and shade diversified,
  Is dear, ay, very dear to thee.

It has been thine to sojourn long
   'Mongst strangers on a foreign strand :
It has been mine to live among
   The mountains of my native land.

It has been thine to find thy sphere
   Where trade and commerce drive apace :
It has been mine to linger where
   The chariot wheels find resting place.

I do not ask of thee if thou
   Possessor art of lands and gold ;
If bright and brighter prospects now
   For thee with future days unfold.

'Tis well thou dost already see
   The welcome fruits of labour hard,
That honest plodding industry
   Is followed with its meet reward.

That in thy peaceful home which lies
   Among the woodlands of the West
Kind sons and daughters round thee rise
   To comfort thee and call thee blest.

But what the joys that gladden now
   When welcome hours of leisure come ?
Say, are they such as thou didst know
   When dwelling in thy Scottish home ?

In times of joy and festive mirth
   The lively dance, say, dost thou share ?
Do young and old then sally forth
   And to the well-swept barn repair ?

And do ye foot it lightly there
   To lively reel and sweet strathspey,
'Till forced to quit enjoyment rare
   By dawning of the coming day ?

Or do ye gather round the hearth
   When nights are long and chill and cold,
To wake the voice of jocund mirth
   When Scotland's stirring tales are told ?

And do ye tell the deeds of those
  Who set Auld Mither Scotland free?
The brave indomitable Bruce—
  The lordly knight of Elderslie!

Oh! surely from a page so bright
  With careless eye ye cannot turn;
Nor can it be ye e'er forget
  To boast of glorious Bannockburn.

Or, further down the stream of time,
  To life again, say, do ye raise
The sufferings, the deeds sublime,
  Of Scotland's covenanting days?

And do ye love and still revere
  The names of many a noble one—
A Renwick young, a brave Argyle,
  M'Kail, Cargill, and Cameron?

And do ye speak of hills and moors
  Where foemen did the wanderers trace?
Of lonely wilds now doubly dear
  And sacred as their resting place?

When Sabbath comes, do ye unto
  Some little belfrey'd church repair,
And homely courtesies renew
  With friend and old acquaintance there?

And do ye gather at the porch
  And by the sanctuary tread?
And round and near the decent church,
  Say, is it there ye lay your dead?

And is the holy table spread
  On Sacramental Sabbath days?
And are the people's praises led
  In simple Psalm and Paraphrase?

And as ye break the holy calm
  When rising from the sacred board,
Say, is it with the well-known Psalm—
  "O thou, my soul, bless God the Lord"?

Yea, when ye go to Zion's hill
  Upon your father's God to call,
Do ye observe and cherish still
  The simple Scottish ritual ?

If thus in foreign lands ye feel
  The influence of Scotland still;
If Scottish customs with you dwell
  And Scottish joys your bosoms thrill ;

Then 'mong the prairies of the west,
  'Mong friends and friendships leal and true,
Of labour, wealth, and lands possessed,
  Oh! surely it is well with you.

For o'er your own dear sea-girt isle
  A dreary shadow long has spread,
And idle thousands seek for toil,
  While children cry in vain for bread.

Nor doth the light begin to dawn,
  Nor speaketh Hope in terms serene ;
Nor breaks the gloomy cloud, nor can
  Its silver lining yet be seen.

But wherefore thus my verse prolong
  With gloomy thoughts—an endless train ?
Accept this rude and nameless song
  I waft to thee across the main.

Harsh though upon the ear it break,
  Rude and untutored though my lay ;
Some happy thoughts may it awake
  Of friends and faces far away.

And when ye meet in social mood,
  Yea, bound by friendship's sacred spell,
See that your country's name ye toast,
  Her legends and her tales ye tell.

And when ye wake the voice of song
  And jovially in chorus join,
Then, lustily and loud and long,
  Sing "Scotland Yet," and "Auld Langsyne."

GOD SAVE OUR SEA-GIRT ISLAND.

God save our sea-girt island !
  Be still our mountain land
Defended and protected
  By His almighty hand,
Who her so long hath sheltered
  'Neath shadow of His wings,
Who is the God of nations,
  Who is the King of kings.

God save our sea-girt island !
  Long may her dwellers be
From pestilence, from famine,
  And civil discord free.
May truth and justice triumph,
  May righteousness still spread,
May commerce duly flourish,
  And may the poor have bread.

God save our sea-girt island !
  And bless her people all—
The humblest in the cottage,
  The lordliest in the hall ;
And brighter still and purer
  May fealty's flame still burn,
To her the crown that weareth,
  And long that crown hath worn.

God save our sea-girt island !
  Let knaves and tyrants know
He bares His arm to hasten
  Oppression's overthrow ;
Fires each pure aspiration
  Of patriotic soul,
That seeks the elevation
  And welfare of the whole.

God save our sea-girt island !
  Be still our mountain land
Defended and protected
  By His almighty hand,

Who her so long hath sheltered
'Neath shadow of His wings,
Who is the God of nations,
Who is the King of kings.

LANGSYNE AMANG THE WEAVERS.

Langsyne amang the weavers o' oor ain auld-fashioned toon,
What couthie cracks, what jibes an' jokes, what rantin' tales
    gaed roun',
When they were met their wabs to beam, in groups o' aught
    or ten,
Or when gather'd in the gloamin' at the smiddy's gable-en'!

The words an' deeds o' leadin' men in countries near an' far,
The prospects o' a lastin' peace, the threats o' comin' war,
They could wi' ease discuss, and facts o' greatest moment
    weigh,
An' future ill or comin' weal could glibly prophecy.

Langsyne amang the weavers there were sober, thoughtfu'
    men,
Whas only wealth was rowth o' books in their wee but-an'-
    ben:
The mists o' ancient history they could wi' ease dispel,
An' licht an' trifling seemed the task when to their hand it
    fell.

An' when the Poets they took up, o' this there was nae en',
It seemed nae minstrel e'er had liv'd o' whilk they didna ken;
Theocritus they could discuss, an' Homer's lofty lays,
An' ither bards that learned men delight to laud an' praise.

O' this translation an' o' that they could the beauties trace,
An' to each honoured name assign its station an' its place;
While Shakespeare, Milton, Goldsmith, Gray, and famous
    Doctor Young,
They could recite wi' keen delight, an' quote wi' ready
    tongue.

Oor Scottish Poets, too, they could dissect wi' meikle skill,
An' mony a kindly word they spak' o' Hogg an' Tannahill ;
While Ramsay, Ferguson, and Scott, they took them a' by
    turns,
But nane o' them gat half the praise they gied to Robbie
    Burns.

The grave Seceedin' elder, crowned wi' locks o' silvery gray,
Had mony a quaint remark to mak', an' pointed thing to say ;
For he had searched its every nook—the kirk an' state
    domain—
An' could the darkest riddles read, an' duty's path make
    plain.
Austere an' stern he seemed to them that did nae better ken,
But at his ain snug ingle end, the kindliest o' men.

Langsyne amang the weavers there were lads mair bent on
    fun,
Wha likit weel a stealthy crack—'twas a' aboot the gun ;
An' boastit how that "pussie" oft sae simply fell their prey,
In some lane spot by loch or wood, whaur "keepers" seldom
    gae.

The scene is sairly changed, alas ! we meet sic men nae
    mair—
The politicians eloquent, the theologians rare—
They 're swept awa', that motley group, there 's no a remnant
    left ;
We never hear o' "weavin' gear," nor yet o' "warp an' weft."

Yet mony a genial mother now a joyfu' dwellin' cheers,
That there did spend her childhood an' her youth's unsullied
    years ;
An' often has the envied seat o' honour been attained
By minds that there wi' meikle care were by fond parents
    trained.

An' leeze me on thae byegane times, for, oh, I likit weel
The blatt'rin o' the shuttle an' the birr o' the pirn wheel ;
An' meikle genial kindness did my youthfu' bosom ken,
Thro' mony a winter's evenin', in the weaver's but-an'-ben.

AULD SCOTLAND'S YELLOW BROOM.

WE welcome thee, thou joyfu' June,
   Wi' days sae licht an' lang,
When thro' the leafy woods resound
   Sae mony a pleasant sang ;
While myriad flowers bestud the bowers
   Surcharged wi' rich perfume ;
But ah, there 's nane among them a'
   Like Scotland's yellow broom.

'Tis sweet to linger in the shade
   Remote frae human ken,
An' list the siller streamlet glide
   Adoun the leafy glen ;
But let me tread the upland height
   Langsyne we used to climb,
When young hearts leaped wi' fond delight
   Amang the yellow broom.

Deep in the woody vale below
   Are flow'rets sweet an' fair,
Wi' petals openin' to the view
   Mair exquisite an' rare ;
But ask me where the memories
   O' happiest moments come ?
Ah, 'tis on yonder sunny braes
   Amang the yellow broom.

A hundred bards ha'e sung its praise,
   In ages past an' gane,
A hundred yet shall proudly raise
   The patriotic strain.
For aye where'er a loyal Scot
   Has found a humble hame,
Warm hearts will join the joyfu' shout—
   Auld Scotland's yellow broom.

I ha'e nae wealth o' lands or gear,
   Owre that I 'll ne'er repine ;
Nae marble fair, nae sculpture rare
   May mark the grave that 's mine ;

But ane wha hauds auld Scotland's name
  Sae sacred an' sae dear,
May fitly claim the yellow broom
  To wave in beauty there!

Yes, let it wave in native grace,
  Aboon the plain green sod,
Where rests a patriot's heart in peace
  Within its lone abode.
Then till the majesty an' dread
  Of the last morn has come,
I'll slumber sweetly 'neath its shade—
  Auld Scotland's yellow broom.

TO A SLEEPING CHILD.

BEAUTIFUL, innocent, rosy, and fair,
In thy sweet cradle bed slumbering there;
Holy and calm, yea, unclouded thy rest,
As the love borne for thee in a fond mother's breast.

Beautiful, innocent, spotless, sin-free,
Are there no angels pure watching o'er thee,
Shedding their fragrance sweet, Heaven's own flowers.
Seeking to consecrate homes such as ours?

Beautiful, innocent, o'er thee I bow,
Tracing the calm on that rare rounded brow,
Wond'ring if sculptor or artist hath e'er
Looked on a picture so pleasant and fair.

Beautiful, innocent, child of our love—
Thou who this babe has sent, Father above,
Grant in Thy faithfulness that we may ever,
Prizing the treasure, praise Thee the kind Giver.

Beautiful, innocent, spotless, sin-free,
Spirits angelic are watching o'er thee,
Shedding their fragrance sweet, Heaven's own flowers.
O, may they consecrate homes such as ours!

THE DEPARTURE OF WINTER AND RETURN OF SPRING.

'Tis past an' gane, the gloomy reign o' Winter stern an
    drear,
Wi' furious blasts an' withering frosts that filled the heart
    wi' fear—
Wi' raging tempests roll'd along, owre wide unfathomed seas,
Intensifying every pang that age or poortith drees.

But now the lingering snawy tints are fadin' fast awa'
Frae Blackhouse' solitary heights and dowie Dollarlaw ;
Frae proud Dundreigh, frae Tinto's dome, and Meldon's
    rocky maze,
Where, 'mid the darkness of the past, the Druid's flame did
    blaze ;

And where the lonely mist-crowned Cairns their solemn
    vigils keep,
The wild bird's cry is heard to wake the solitude so deep ;
'Mong scenes where towering snowy wreaths like rival
    mountains rose,
The fleecy flocks now roam at will, or peacefully repose.

Now joyously the sunbeams kiss Cardon and Culterfell,
Where erst the simple psalm of praise did up their valleys
    swell,
When ane * wha saw before him placed the martyr's bitter
    cup
Did point to Him who on the throne was high and lifted up;

---

* Holmes Common was a favourite resort of Donald Cargill, the famous
field preacher. On the last occasion on which he preached there, which
was only a few months before his execution, he spoke on the 6th chapter
of Isaiah, where the Almighty is spoken of as "sitting upon a throne
high and lifted up"; and also on Romans xi. 20. "The scene," says
Mr Whitfield, "was sublime and impressive beyond description.
He drew his illustrations from the hills that surrounded them like
bulwarks of defence, with Cardon and Culterfell lifting their kingly
heads above the rest far up into the clouds. He was drawing
near the close of his life, and a foreboding of his coming martyrdom
tinged his thoughts and words with a prophetic power that gave him a
strange fascination over his audience. Six weeks later and the voice
that awakened the mountian echoes of the solitudes of Glenholm was to
be lifted up for the last time upon the uplands of Dunsyre, and to
bear its dying testimony in the Grassmarket of Edinburgh."

Or, standing on the heathy banks of Holmes' pure infant
    stream,
Declared His love was found of those who sought not after
    Him.

How dear ye are! ye heath clad hills that proudly round
    us rise,
With scenery rich and varied like your mingled memories,
Yet fairest do ye seem by far when wintry storms give way,
And earth rejoiceth in the smile of April and of May.

Thrice welcome then, thou joyfu' Spring, wi' days sae licht
    an' lang,
Wi' burstin' buds, wi' openin' flowers, an' mony a mellow
    sang,
And when the velvet sward sae green wi' lichtsome foot
    we 've prest,
We feel sweet Hope renew her reign ance mair within the
    breast.

CARGILL'S LAST SERMON.

Verses occasioned by a visit to Dunsyre Common, where the celebrated field preacher, Donald Cargill, preached on the last day of his liberty, his text on that memorable occasion being the words in Isaiah xxvi. 20 and 21—"Come, my people, enter thou into thy chambers, and shut thy doors about thee: hide thyself as it were for a little moment, until the indignation be overpast. For, behold, the Lord cometh out of his place to punish the inhabitants of the earth for their iniquity; the earth also shall disclose her blood, and shall no more cover her slain." A reward of 5000 merks being offered, Cargill was apprehended the following morning at the house of Mr Fisher of Covington Mill, by Irving of Bonshaw and a company of dragoons. The rough and contemptuous treatment he received, and the events that intervened between the capture and his execution in the Grassmarket of Edinburgh are too well known to require rehearsal.

AND do I pace the peaceful spot
    Where that undaunted champion stood,
And fearlessly God's people taught
    While tyrants thirsted for his blood?

And are those lone, blue hills the last
    That did unto his voice resound?
Ah! surely then this desert waste
    Is more than consecrated ground.

And were the eager listeners here
   Around the noble preacher ranged
In this grand amphitheatre
   That still remaineth all unchanged ?

And did he speak as 'neath the shade
   Of that sad martyrdom so near ?
Ah ! surely then for me 'tis good
   That I should pause and ponder here—

When vividly before me rise
   The lives of true and trusty men,
The tale of whose self-sacrifice
   Makes sacred many a moorland glen ;

Men who did drink the cup of woe
   And braved the scaffold and the steel,
That Scotland's sons might share and know
   The highest freedom—holiest weal.

Let others love the battle-field,
   The scenes of carnage and of war,
And join with those who have extolled
   The victor and the conqueror ;

Yet is not oft the joyful shout
   That fills the air and rends the sky
But hushed, and then we hear aloud
   The widow's wail, the orphan's cry ?

And are not oft those glorious deeds,
   Whose record history proudly saves,
The work of men who are indeed
   Of fouler lusts the helpless slaves ?

Ah ! dear to me the moorland glens
   Where foemen did those wanderers chase,
The mist-crowned hills, the caves and dens,
   That often proved their hiding-place.

From tyrants who, though armed with power
   To torture, slay, and trample down,
Yet could not scathe the golden dower,
   The victor's palm or martyr's crown,

Or stem the tide of free-born thought,
  Which from their time has freely spread,
A heritage right dearly bought,
  A testimony sealed with blood,

Which shall its wholesome influence lend
  Among the homes on Scotia's shore,
Till history's latest page is penned,
  And time itself shall be no more.

Strange that while here all their reward
  Was ceaseless toil and sufferings,
Whose memory we now regard
  The dearest of all earthly things;

For names that once were rudely stained
  With foul reproach of blackest brand,
Are now in generous hearts enshrined,
  The glory of our Covenant land.

And do I pace the peaceful spot
  Where that undaunted champion stood,
And fearlessly God's people taught
  While tyrants thirsted for his blood ?

And are those lone blue hills the last
  That did unto his voice resound ?
Ah ! surely then this desert waste
  Is more than consecrated ground.

OOR AIN GEAN TREE.

Richt bonny owre the burn it hings, oor ain gean tree,
An' lo'esome are its flourishings, oor ain gean tree ;
It seems amaist as winsome yet as when we a' were wee
An' singin' blithely 'neath its shade—oor ain gean tree.

It bounds oor bonny garden green, oor ain gean tree,
An' stan's the burn an' it atween, oor ain gean tree ;
The streamlet's sang is sweet, I ween, but let me hear the glee
O' mony youthfu' voices 'neath oor ain gean tree.

O, mony a summer it has seen, oor ain gean tree,
An' mony a bonny autumn moon, oor ain gean tree;
An' may the day be distant far when we nae mair shall see
The gracefu' siller blossoms o' oor ain gean tree.

Richt dear to hearts noo far away, oor ain gean tree,
Aneath its shade wha used to play, oor ain gean tree;
The half o' a' their gowd an' gear there's some wad gladly gie
To spend ae simmer's gloamin' near oor ain gean tree.

Richt aften hae I sung its praise, oor ain gean tree,
In nameless rhymes and artless lays, oor ain gean tree;
Ah, only when death's downy sleep at last has closed my e'e,
An' ne'er till then, can I forget oor ain gean tree.

BURNS' COTTAGE.

Verses written on visiting the above, along with a few friends; and suggested by reading the ticket near the bed, requesting visitors not to touch anything.

NAY, we shall not these relics touch
    With rash and sacrilegious hand;
They tell of him whose lays enrich
    The dwellings of our mountain land.

Far dearer than the diadem
    That decks the proudest monarch's brow,
Those simple things around, which claim
    Our rapt and fond attention now.

The lowly roof 'neath which we stand
    And linger with uncovered head,
The humble hearth we now surround—
    And homely floor on which we tread,

Are match'd by no baronial pile
    That boldly doth its turrets rear;
No lordly hall on Scottish soil
    To Scottish bosoms half so dear.

From morn till eve—from year to year—
　　The pilgrims come—the pilgrims go ;
No vulgar revel pains the ear,
　　No railer's voice heard here, O no !

But gentle whispers, soft and low,
　　And kindly words alone are heard
When gazing on the couch of straw
　　Where he was born—our Peasant Bard.

And many a mingled feeling here
　　To life within the bosom starts,
When parting from the scenes so dear
　　To true and loving Scottish hearts.

It may be long ere we return
　　To stand where we to-day have stood,
When brightly in each breast did burn
　　The kindly flame of brotherhood,

To stroll alang the banks o' Ayr,
　　Or by the Doon's dear waters stray ;
Or scan with scrutinizing care
　　The ruins of Kirk Alloway :

But through Life's future years or hours,
　　With chequered lot or mingled cup,
Those memories must be crowned with flowers
　　Which this bright day has treasured up.

Nay, we shall not those relics touch
　　With rash and sacrilegious hand,
That tell of him whose lays enrich
　　The dwellings of our mountain land.

Far dearer than the diadem
　　That decks the proudest monarch's brow,
Those simple things around, which claim
　　Our rapt and fond attention now.

No fierce proud force of armed men,
　　No iron bars their safety prove ;
More powerful their protection when
　　Defended by a nation's love.

SCOTLAND YET

Verses written on reading of the unveiling of the Burns Statue in London, and the address by the Earl of Rosebery on that occasion.

AYE now and then there comes the time
When glows afresh the genial flame
O' love for mither Scotland's name,
  Our mountain land,
Whose heroes on the roll of fame
  The foremost stand.

Ev'n now a simple son of toil—
The maist obscure on Scottish soil—
Proud o' the lad was born in Kyle,
  Exultant hears ;
What coming frae the sister isle
  His bósom cheers.

An' shall my lowly muse decline
To share the pride an' joy that's mine,
Or prompt for me the measured line ?
  I vow an' swear
That I, henceforth, the muses' shrine
  Shall seek nae mair.

'Tis true we ken that dukes an' lords
Are oft a blast o' idle words,
Wham every thoughtfu' man regards
  As meaning little ;
Yet now we see there may be lords
  Worthy the title.

Yes, Rosebery, ye ha'e e'en dune weel,
Three cheers for thee, thou spunky chiel ;
Thy wit, thy lear, thy tact an' skill,
  We kent that's true,
But never lo'ed thee half sae weel
  As we do noo.

C

Wi' skilfu' hand an' kindly word
Ye waked a sympathetic chord
When o' oor ain dear peasant bard
      Ye spak' sae fairly ;
Sic manly sentiments are heard
      But very rarely.

Wi' willin' hands we twine anew
The laurel for thy noble brow ;
Thy name—that is nae stranger now
      On fame's bright pages—
Shall yet wi' brighter lustre glow
      In coming ages.

A thocht is often in my head,
It's e'en a pity Burns is dead :
Had he in this, oor time o' need—
      Been here amang us—
He wad hae gien the loons a screed
      That seek to wrang us.

In satire keen, in burning line,
In language faithfu' mair than fine,
He wad hae bared each deep design
      An' shown them fully.
We mind what "Hornbook" gat langsyne,
      An' "Holy Willie."

We've Holy Willies 'mang us still,
An' Hornbooks too, we ken that weel ;
What's waur, loons that wi' a' their skill
      Withhold what's due
Frae them o' whilk Burns cam' himsel'—
      Is that na true ?

An' when our present situation
Receives our calm consideration,
It's e'en a wild an' weird sensation
      That thrills the breast ;
If it's na righteous indignation,
      Then what else is 't ?

For tho' we be persuaded, fully,
That time will yet disclose their folly,
Upsetting a' their vain unholy
   Insinuations ;
Yet tedious delays—weel, truly,
   They try oor patience.

Had it been some wee ripplin' rill
Windin' around the lonely hill,
An' wanderin' amaist at will
   In dubious course,
They might hae better proved their skill
   Near its weak source.

But to attempt to stem a river
Whose gathering waves are resting never,
More stately and majestic ever
   Nearer the main ;
O, sic a hoax ! O, what a haver !
   How rash and vain !

Yet 'mid the struggle that remains,
Let ilka ane use a' his pains
While friendship binds an' union reigns
   Now and throughout,
Like laws o' Medes and Persians
   That alter not.

An' when I neist my lyre shall wake
For freedom and for Scotland's sake,
May it be as the shadows break
   An' pass away,
An' mony a glorious gowden streak
   Foretells the day.

That day a joyfu' jubilee,
When labour's honest sons shall be
Frae serfdom's latest shred set free,
   Stigma and stain ;
An' when the draught they blithely pree,
   It 's but their ain.

Success to thee, Dalmeny, still,
An' a' wha seek auld Scotland's weal,
By pen or sword, or pointed steel—
    As oft we've read it—
Wha' for her sake wad face the deil
    If that were needed.

An' though for Burns ye bauldly claim
The highest pinnacle of fame,
Thinkna, thereby, your ain fair name
    Has ought to fear;
Nay, it maun be through comin' time
    Held doubly dear.

THE AULD LINT MILL.*

From the author's first volume, by special request of a few friends.

AIR—"Kelvin Grove."

LET me linger on the brae by the Auld Lint Mill,
At the peacefu' close o' day by the Auld Lint Mill;
    Let me list the torrent's din,
    Rushing down the deep ravine,
There to meet the limpid Lyne by the Auld Lint Mill.

The valley, oh, how dear, round the Auld Lint Mill,
And each sight an' scene that's near to the Auld Lint Mill!
    Let the pleasin' past declare
    O' the happy moments there,
That return to me nae mair, by the Auld Lint Mill.

For how often did we play 'round the Auld Lint Mill,
In our youth's delightfu' day by the Auld Lint Mill,
    When our hearts were fou o' glee,
    As the warblers on the tree,
Or the lambkins sportin' free 'round the Auld Lint Mill!

* An old ruin on the banks of the Lyne, a mile above the village of Linton, and now a favourite resort of summer visitors. The romantic scenery has been transferred to the canvas, of late, by artists—amateur and professional.

Though my playmates now are far frae the Auld Lint Mill,
And though some will look nae mair on the Auld Lint Mill,
    Every face and every name
    Dwells in memory's page the same,
Though I dinna meet wi' them by the Auld Lint Mill.

Then the praises I will sing o' the Auld Lint Mill,
Till the lonely woods shall ring 'round the Auld Lint Mill,
    An' the gladsome glittering stream
    Shall re-echo back the hymn,
'Neath the gloamin' shades sae dim 'round the Auld Lint
    Mill.

ANNIE GONE FOR EVER.

BREEZES of the balmy eve,
    Zephyrs softly sighing,
Whisper gently o'er the grave
    Where a loved one's lying.
By yon fair and flowery thorn
    Holy angels hover,
Round the spot where many mourn
    Annie gone for ever.

Closèd now those eyes of blue,
    Once that beamed so brightly ;
Still'd for aye those fairy feet,
    Once that tripped so lightly.
Shrouded now that snow white brow
    In death's chamber lonely,
Where those lips lie closed that spoke
    Words of kindness only.

We will plant about thy head
    Flowers of Spring the rarest,
We will strew around thy bed
    Summer blooms the fairest,
Types of thee and of thy fate,
    Sweet, though faded roses,
Shall be scattered round the spot
    Where thy dust reposes.

Breezes of the balmy eve,
　　Zephyrs softly sighing,
Whisper gently o'er the grave
　　Where a loved one's lying.
By yon fair and flowery thorn
　　Holy angels hover,
Round the spot where many mourn
　　Annie gone for ever.

VERSES ON THE BATTLE OF CULLODEN.

Fought on 16th April, 1746.

Fourteen of the Pretender's banners were brought to Edinburgh ; an
by the Duke of Cumberland's command, those banners, which had
spread terror over a great part of the island, were burned with every mark
of contempt and ignominy. The heralds, trumpeters &c., escorted the
common executioner, who carried the Pretender's colours, and thirteen
chimney-sweepers, who carried the rest of the colours, from the castle to
the cross. They were burned one by one, an herald always proclaiming
the names of the commanders to which the respective colours belonged.
　　　　　　　　　　　—*Arnot's History of Edinburgh.*

WAKE the pibroch ! wake the pibroch ! weird and woeful be
　　its wail,
Let its shrillest shrieks be wafted on the fitful April gale.
'Tis a tale with sorrow laden ! 'tis a dirge of deepest woe !
hat we wake for thee, Culloden ! where the valiant wer'Te
　　laid low.

Wake the pibroch ! wake the pibroch ! not the rallying
　　battle cry,
With the tartaned clansmen gathering, and the banners
　　floating high.
They are gone now—gone for ever, the bright banners that
　　they bore !
And the stalwart clansmen rally round their gallant chiefs
　　no more.

Wake the pibroch ! sound the slogan ! let their glory not go
　　down,
Though we mourn not that the Stuart never more shall wear
　　the crown.

Yet we love thee, lone Culloden ! where the valiant found a
    grave,
As we cherish still the memory of the noble, true, and brave.

Wake the pibroch ! sound the slogan ! thro' the lonely
    Highland glen !
Bid us dream again of Drummond, of Lord Murray and his
    men !
Feel again those strange emotions thro' the bosom flit and
    steal
At the mention of Clanranald, of Glengarry and Lochiel.

Wake the pibroch ! wake the pibroch ! ere we bid a last
    farewell
To the spot where he did listen to his clansmen's funeral
    knell,
Ere he braved those deeds of daring by the mountain and
    the wave,
That enshrine the name for ever of the Royal Fugitive.

Wake the pibroch ! wake the pibroch ! weird and woeful be
    its wail,
Let its shrillest shrieks be wafted on the fitful April gale.
'Tis a tale with sorrow laden ! 'tis a dirge of deepest woe !
That we wake for thee, Culloden ! where the valiant were
    laid low.

OOR TAM.

A PITY oor Tam's sic a terrible loon—
Sic a wild steerin', rough tearin', terrible loon,
He's brocht me to grief noo wi' half o' the toon ;
A pity oor Tam's sic a terrible loon.

There's nae kind o' tricks that oor Tam doesna try,
Nae mischief but he has a hand i' the pie,
Nae reckless adventure, an' nae noisy splore,
But Tam's aye the leader an' king o' the core.

Whene'er on the streets there's a wild drunken brawl,
A row or a racket 'mang young folks or aul' ;
When there's bees' bykes to plunder, or kitlens to droon,
Ye'll find oor Tam there—he's a terrible loon.

Gif I choose him a task, swift awa' frae 't he steals,
An' aff to the fishin' for perches or eels,
An' no' till the sun owre the hill has gaen doon
Will we see oor Tam's face—he 's a terrible loon.

In vain ha'e I tried to keep claes on his back,
The best I can buy dinna stand him a crack—
As a rule Tam is ne'er at a loss to compete
Wi' the warst ragamuffin that rins i' the street.

Complaints frae the neebors are serious and rife,
Lang screeds frae his teachers—they worry my life—
Braid hints frae the police o' what maun be done
Wi' that laddie Tam—he 's a terrible loon.

Some aulder folks chide me, an' warn me to wait,
That wisdom and wit shall ae day fill his pate;
I wish I could share in thae prospects sae bricht,
They 've been lang on the road and they 're no yet in sicht.

I look at him whiles when he 's laid doon to sleep,
When wandering thochts through my bosom will creep:
Will he no be cared for by Ane that 's aboon!
For kind, kind 's oor Tam, though a terrible loon.

A pity oor Tam 's sic a terrible loon—
Sic a wild steerin, rough tearin', terrible loon,
He 's brocht me to grief wi' the half o' the toon—
A pity oor Tam 's sic a terrible loon.

EPISTLE TO MR ALEXANDER BRUNTON OF INVERKEITHING.

Mr Brunton, to whom the following was addressed nearly four years ago, was born at Newburgh on Tay, in 1805; and in his limited education and early application to labour, bore a close resemblance to many of our most eminent men whose memories are held in grateful remembrance. His education terminated when he was only in his ninth year; and at the immature age of sixteen he was engaged in active labour in the quarries of his native district. From childhood he evinced a keen desire for historical reading, and a love for the Latin language, which he set himself assiduously to study, and of which he by and by became master, enabling him to read in the original many works which were of great value to him in after life, when studying the life and daring deeds of the great Scottish hero.

Mr Brunton's first appearance in print was at the erection of the Wallace Monument twenty-eight years ago, when he made a powerful and vigorous reply to some hostile and adverse criticism that then found place in the prints. Ever since that time he has been recognised as a valuable authority on this and other historical matters, and the work published by him on "The Life and Heroic Actions of Sir William Wallace" has enjoyed a wide circulation. In private life Mr Brunton was known as a man of retiring disposition and diligent business habits, spending his leisure hours in the bosom of an affectionate family. Many literary men of no inconsiderable note were proud to be honoured with his friendship, and now recall with pleasure many happy hours spent in the company of one whose noble presence was so much in keeping with his tastes and pursuits. His death took place on 12th May, 1887.

You'll pardon, sir, my dull delay,
When I take up my pen this day
A just and honest debt to pay
   In rhyming mood,
And thereby unto thee convey
   My gratitude.

The brief but happy interview,
When lately, sir, I spoke wi' you,
On Scotia's noble sons and true
   O deathless fame ;
Wi' a' the kindness ye did show,
   Demands the same.

The little beuk that bears your name,
I've carefully perused the same ;
Nor lazy ha'e ye been nor lame—
   Searchin' an' siftin'
Through a'thing that concerns his fame,
   That glorious chieftain.

Nae myth that moody minds create,
As some would oft insinuate—
A being, noble, generous, great,
   Worthy the Giver,
Whose memory destined is by fate
   To live for ever !

A noble undertaking thine,
An' patriotic in design,
Around his brow, man, steive to twine
  The laurel wreath,
Wha lo'ed Auld Scotland's sons langsyne
  Unto the death.

Beloved his name maun ever be
While Scotia's rivers seek the sea,
An' mountain streams glide merrily
  The glens amang ;
Renowned alike in history
  An' deathless sang.

Thir twa three verses now I string
To ane o' them wha's praise I sing,
Wha honour to Auld Scotland bring
  On every shore ;
While Robbie Burns himsel' is king
  O' a' the core.

The stalwart sons o' honest toil,
Wha 'mid their labours seek the while,
Alike 'neath fortune's frown and smile,
  Wi' zeal an' patience,
To raise our ancient Scottish isle
  High 'mang the nations.

Lang may 't be sao ; lang may they prove
Their honest an' deep-rooted love
To beuks an' lear, an' onward move,
  Progressing fast,
Through coming ages, as they have
  Throughout the past.

Intelligently may they still
Seek to promote the nation's weal,
An' prove, while they exert their skill
  An' promptly meddle,
That armed men an' pointed steel
  Play second fiddle.

I canna say I envy sair
They wha possess baith gowd and gear ;
They 're often nane the happier
   O' a' they ha'e,
While wealth aft proves a deadly snare
   To mony mae.

But I confess I envy them
Wha store their minds frae time to time
Wi' histories o' deeds sublime
   An' usefu' knowledge,
Whereby they aften put to shame
   Men trained at college.

Lang may 't be thine to ponder o'er
The rich an' interesting store
O' quaint an' antiquated lore
   Which thou canst boast ;
Result o' neither little care
   Nor little cost.

Lang may ye pen the pithy line
Owre Scotland's heroes o' langsyne,
Within the joyfu' hame that 's thine,
   'Mid a' thing dear ;
While son and dochter, wife and wean,
   Thy bosom cheer.

An' let me say, when I return
To Culross or to Torryburn,
Or to Dumfarlin' tak a turn,
   I 'll seek a breathin'
Where friendship's flame doth brichtly burn,
   At Inverkeithin'.

An' frae my cheerie cronies there
I 'll surely find twa hours to spare,
To hae a rantin' crack an' rare
   Wi' ane sae zealous
That nane shall harm a single hair
   O' Willie Wallace.

Your little beuk will doubtless claim
A place in mony a Scottish hame ;
An' far ayont the ocean's faem,
   Whaure'er they 're placed,
Auld Scotland's sons, 'twill be wi' them
   A welcome guest.

An' noo, my cantie, couthie chiel,
I 'll for the present say fareweel ;
But be assured o' this, that while
   This heart keeps duntin',
Aft owre the Forth my thochts shall steal
   To honest Brunton.

An' while the joyous Summer reigns
Owre Scotland's fair and fertile plains,
An' mony a nameless bard attunes
   His lowly lyre,
Accept these rude, untutored strains
   Frae Peeblesshire.

WITHERED LIKE THE AUTUMN LEAF.

A poor woman who had suddenly lost her husband by a railway accident, in describing her feelings, said she could not cry, she felt as if " withered and dried like a leaf."

WITHERED and dried like the sere autumn leaf,
Yea, thus did I feel in the depth of my grief,
When Death's ruthless hand on my partner did fall,
As I trembled and cowered 'neath his dark sombre pall.
With my children around me, left fatherless all.

Withered and dried like the sere autumn leaf.
Ah ! mine was the sorrow that sought not relief
In wild cries of anguish, in fierce floods of tears,
The gloomy forebodings, the heart-rending fears
That hung like a cloud o'er my life's future years.

Withered and dried like the sere autumn leaf,
Yet, well-known to One was my unspoken grief ;
He who said, " Peace, be still," gave me grace to obey,
'Mid the unspoken anguish of that awful day,
And in Him do I find now my shield and my stay.

GLENCOE.

Verses written on reading a full account of the massacre of its inhabitants, which took place on the tempestuous morning of the 16th February, 1692.

How woeful and weird still the heart-stirring story,
 That oft in life's morning, now long, long ago,
We pondered and sighed o'er the deeds foul and gory,
 That sounded the death-knell of lonely Glencoe.

O! dire dreadful scene, dark'ning history's pages,
 Black record of treachery, terror, and pain,
Defying the wisdom and skill of the ages
 To change by one shadow that unchanging stain.

How sad the lone wail that did reach thee, Con Fion,*
 Ere the smoke from the valley rose darkly and slow,
That told how the foul bloody task of Glenlyon,
 Was bloodily sealed in the lonely Glencoe!

Majestic proud Malmor,* ah! didst thou not listen
 The jubilant shouts of his barbarous men,
When the cold wintry sun on the scene had arisen
 And lit up the gloom of the desolate glen?

And thou, widowed Cona,* do not thy dark waters
 Bemoan the brave clansmen, as onward they flow,
And mourn the dark doom of fair innocent daughters,
 That sleep 'neath the ruins of lonely Glencoe?

Should I ever gaze on thy dark frowning mountains,
 O, let it not be when the spring flowers are nigh,
Nor when summer's bright sun lights the lakes and the
  fountains,
 Or autumn's sere leaves in the lonely wood lie.

Ah! no; let it be when the tempest is sweeping
 'Mid the hurricane's wrath and the cold blinding snow,
As it swept when the weak and the helpless were weeping
 When sharing the dire dreadful doom of Glencoe.

* Con Fion and Malmor are the names of two hills, the one on the north, the other on the south, while Cona is the name of the stream that winds down the depth of the valley of Glencoe.

O, Scotland! dear land of the rock and the wildwood,
   The lake and the river, the glen and the grove;
Thy history, how dear since the days of my childhood!
   Thy minstrels, how worthy the heart's warmest love!

But, ah! no fond feeling of proud exultation,
   Glencoe, can thy mem'ries for us ever boast;
Still thou liv'st in the righteous and fierce indignation
   That burns for thee still in the patriot's breast.

Yet thy doom like the roll of Ezekiel written
   Within and without "lamentation and woe,"
The last and the awful tribunal awaiting
   Shall then all its guilt and full penalty know.

BEAUTIFUL MAY.

BEAUTIFUL morning in beautiful May,
Welcome, thrice welcome, thy gladdening ray.
Now, when the tempests of Winter are o'er,
Now, when the Spring's chilling blasts are no more,
Welcome, thrice welcome, thy gladdening ray,
Beautiful morning in beautiful May.

Beautiful morning in beautiful May,
Chasing the mists from the blue hills away,
When the calm lakelets and clear bounding streams
Sparkle and dance 'neath thy glorious beams,
Lighting the moorland, the valley and strath,
Scattering flowers by the lone mountain path,
Where, in our childhood, so oft we did stray,
Beautiful morning in beautful May.

Beautiful morning in beautiful May,
Calm is thy dawn on the sweet Sabbath day,
Deeper, then deeper, the silence that reigns
'Mong the wild mountains, and o'er the wide plains,
When up the hill-side, and down the deep dell,
Steals the sweet chime of the church-going bell,
Laden with memories holy and dear,
Fragrant with hopes that bring heaven so near,
Welcome withal, as in life's early day,
Beautiful morning in beautiful May.

Beautiful morning, in beautiful May,
Welcome, thrice welcome, thy gladdening ray,
Now, when the tempests of Winter are o'er,
Now, when the Spring's chilling blasts are no more,
Now, when the woods, fields, and hedge-rows are seen
Robed in their brightest and liveliest green,
Welcome, thrice welcome, thy gladdening ray,
Beautiful morning in beautiful May.

RETURN, O LORD; HOW LONG ? *

THE thought that often filled my heart, the words my lips
did know,
When first the dreary shadow fell, ten long, long years ago,
When by the fair and fading form of one both near and
dear
I watch'd by night and day, while oft I shed the hidden
tear ;
And while the shadow rested still, for weeks, for months,
and years,
I struggled on through fading hopes, I cried 'mid gathering
fears,
Thou who dost fill our humble home with sorrow, not with
song,
O, let Thy presence pierce the gloom—" Return, O Lord,
how long ? "

* In a quiet secluded spot in the valley of the Esk stands a little cluster of cottages within a mile of the mansion of Sir George Douglas Clerk of Penicuik, viz., Corntown Cottages. One of these has been the scene of very protracted family affliction and trying breavement, the family we refer to being that of Mr Napier, shepherd. In 1873, Katherine, his daughter, took ill and lay in bed for ten years, her death taking place in April 1883, at the age of 33. During the period of Katherine's illness, viz., in 1879, Nelly took ill and died in May 1880, aged 25. During the same period Mary also took ill, viz., in 1882, and died in September, 1883, at the age of 17. It will thus be seen that for many years there were seldom less than two cases of severe illness in the dwelling at one time, and many of the records of those dark days in the history of a family well known and very much respected, are of the saddest and most painful character, and have called forth the warmest sympathies of the thoughtful portion of the community generally, as well as of their immediate friends. The above verses were sent anonymously to Mrs Napier. The closing lines refer to John Napier, a brother of the three sisters, whose death took place at the early age of 22, only a few days after the above lines were written.

And when the river of our grief in wider waves did flow,
And in our humble home we saw another form laid low,
Amid the strange bewilderment that then the bosom knew,
When thoughts were sad and many; ay, and words were
     brief and few,
The thought was near me when their eyes with gentle hand
     I closed,
And looked upon the faded form that then in death reposed,
And when a weary wanderer those doleful shades among,
The plaint oft reached my Father's ear—"Return, O Lord:
     how long?"

And was the fiery trial past, and was the spoiler stayed,
When two young forms were side by side in the lone church-
     yard laid?
Ah! no, 'twas ours to drink anew the bitter cup of woe,
And see within our humble home another form laid low,
To watch another sufferer with meekness bow the head,
And mark the fell destroyer come with slow but certain
     tread,
And when the spoiler's shafts flew thrice, and thrice my
     peace was slain,
And this lone bosom yearned o'er those that did with me
     remain,
Amid the deepest darkness of that terrible eclipse
Back came the simple litany unto my trembling lips,
When saddest memories, darkest fears, did by my pathway
     throng,
I only cried, amid my tears, "Return, O Lord; how long?"

And yet the shadow hovers still, and yet it is my fate,
Beside the bed of a dear son with weary heart to wait.
May He who gave me grace and strength to stand the evil
     day
And bow the head when He did call earth's dearest ones
     away,
He who to me has granted strength through all the painful
     past,
Oh may He guide me till I cross the Jordan's wave at last.
I know not if the memories of all our partings here
Shall reach us in that better land and yonder radiant sphere.

One thing I know, they shall not mar the glories of the
    blest,
Nor cast one dim, brief shadow, in that dear, dear land of
    rest ;
And when we stand around the throne and join the angel's
    song,
Then shall the plaint no more be known—"Return, oh Lord;
    how long ?"

THE BURN THAT WHILES RINS DRY.

It has its source the meads amang
    By yon lone woodland wide,
Where first is heard the cuckoo's sang
    In a' the kintra side ;
It skirts the base o' nae proud hill
    Or mountain towerin' high,
But wimples doon its nameless dell—
    The burn that whiles rins dry.

Its glassy waves are ne'er o'erlook'd
    By grand baronial tower,
They seek in nae lone leafy nook
    My lord or lady's bower ;
But busy farm and cottage hame
    It wimples gladly by,
Where blithesome bairns its waters stem—
    The burn that whiles rins dry.

We've seen 't o'erspread its banks and braes
    When cam' the Spring-time thaws,
An' oft when we in Autumn days
    Were gatherin' o' the haws ;
We too hae seen Sol's scorching beam
    Its fountain sairly try,
An' lend it that sad luckless name—
    The burn that whiles rins dry.

Yet bonnie spots bestud its braes
    When whins are a' in bloom,
As aft we've seen in youth's bright days,
    When wand'rin' 'mang the broom ;

D

Bright seemed the joyous future then,
  And hopes were pure and high,
And gladsome seemed its bonnie glen—
  The burn that whiles rins dry.

Is there nae moral in the sang
  That bonnie burnie sings—
Nae strange mysterious murmuring
  Of frail and fleeting things?
Does it nae bid us fix our love
  On things that are on high—
And warn us that earth's joys oft prove
  A burn that whiles rins dry?

THE PRESENT, AND THE FUTURE.

WHY do we ponder on the past
  For ever and for aye,
As if no shadow e'er o'ercast
  The sunshine of its day;
As if no failing and no fault
  Upon its pages shone;
As if life's path were then bestrewn
  With flowers, and flowers alone?

Why do we ponder on the past?
  It had its sunshine—true;
Ay, but it had its griefs and fears,
  And days of darkest hue.
Although, perhaps, 'tis well that these
  From memory's page we blot,
The sunshine all remembered, but
  The shadows all forgot.

Why do we ponder on the past
  With meaningless regret?
Perhaps the present is to us
  With brighter diamonds set.
And ills that once within the breast
  Waked terror and alarm,
We meet with more unflinching front,
  And brave with stronger arm.

Why do we ponder on the past?
  The memories of its hours
Are radiant of the golden time
  Of buds and opening flowers.
But now we drink the deeper draught
  Of pleasures more sublime,
Befitting more the strength and pride
  Of manhood's stalwart prime.

Why do we ponder on the past?
  Yea, why not turn away
A keen and eager glance to cast
  Into life's future day?
While higher aspirations our
  Imaginations fire,
And purer thoughts, and holier aims,
  Our breasts and lives inspire.

'Tis thus successfully we'll chase
  Our present cares away,
And of a lasting future peace
  The sure foundation lay.
Thus sweeter memories shall we store
  For days that are to come,
And brighter make the pathway when
  We're nearer to our home.

THE QUAINT OLD PICTURE.

Spare for me that quaint old picture in the corner of my
    room,
Let no rash or reckless fingers near the sacred relic come;
Be its outlines faint and feeble, its adornments very plain,
Yet I charge thee that the treasure all unchanged with me
    remain.
Fruit of warm and fond affection more than rare artistic
    skill,
Work of heart and hands now resting in the churchyard
    lone and still,
That from lov'd ones oft has courted many a fond and
    lingering gaze,
Bound thou art unto this bosom, in a thousand tender ways.

Spare for me the quaint old picture, for it leads my thoughts
    away
Back unto the home of childhood—back to youth's delight-
    ful day.
'Tis my own dear father's father, with that noble brow and
    grand,
Who so often in life's morning led me fondly by the hand,
Speaking words of warmest kindness as we strayed beside
    the stream,
While the tiny teardrop often in his aged eye did gleam,
As he fanned my brow so gently, as he stroked my locks of
    gold,
While a bright and happy future he so lovingly foretold.

Spare for me the quaint old picture, let it still be very near—
It may wake for me the accents of that voice I loved to hear
In the psalm of praise at even, in the holy chapters read,
And the faithful prayers he offered, ah, how reverently said!
It may reproduce the faces and the forms that round him
    knelt,
Bid me feel for one brief moment as in youth's bright morn
    I felt,
E'en though thoughts that are the saddest follow swiftly in
    their train,
As I think upon the remnants of that band that now
    remain.

Spare for me the quaint old picture; do not let it be dis-
    placed
From the corner where so closely I those features oft have
    traced.
It has been my mute companion now through many chang-
    ing years,
In the times of joyous sunshine, in the days of doubts and
    fears.
Rich and many are the memories that it still unto me brings,
Let me part with it, yes, only with all other earthly things,
When those forms to me the dearest swiftly from my vision
    fade,
And as swiftly do the shadows of the long night o'er me
    spread.

Spare for me that quaint old picture in the corner of my
　　room,
Let no rash or reckless fingers near the sacred relic come :
Be its outlines faint and feeble, its adornments very plain ;
Yet I charge thee that the treasure all unchanged with me
　　remain.

A DAY IN YARROW.

A DAY in Yarrow! happy thought,
　　Though happier thoughts shall waken
When we ascend the lonely height,
　　Through heather and through bracken,
The beauteous landscape there to trace,
　　Whose hill-tops, crowned with glory,
Rise up 'mong scenes whose names find place
　　In dear and deathless story.

A day in Yarrow! be it ours,
　　When May her flower-wreath bringeth,
Or when among June's leafy bowers
　　The mellow blackbird singeth ;
Nor laverock's song, nor blackbird's lay,
　　Shall prove a dirge of sorrow,
Nor shall the lovely flowers of May
　　Less lovely seem in Yarrow.

A day in Yarrow, when her waves
　　'Neath sunbeams bright are straying,
And lesser streams their margins lave,
　　To her their tribute paying.
No tale of woe to thrill us now,
　　Waked by her winding waters,
But breathing loves, both leal and true,
　　'Mong her own sons and daughters.

Dear is the heath and soft green sward,
　　The streamlet's sweet meander,
Where often Ettrick's mountain bard
　　In solitude did wander,
When gazing on her glens and streams
　　So classic and so lonely,

Enwrapt in those mysterious dreams
  Known to him and him only.

A day among the "Dowie Dens,"
  Where Wordsworth sought and found him,
With minstrelsey of Borderland,
  Like mantle wrapt around him.
They wandered there as in a dream,
  Enchanter and enchanted,
'Neath cloudlet dim and rainbow's rim,
  From fairyland transplanted.

A day among the forest scenes,
  By no dark cloud belated;
For comfort, peace, and gladness reigns
  Where Flodden desolated.
And rich and rare the garland fair
  The muses chose to weave her,
Of plaintive song, both sweet and pure,
  Song that shall live for ever.

A day in Yarrow! happy thought,
  Though happier thoughts shall waken
When we ascend the lonely height
  Through heather and through bracken,
The beauteous landscape there to trace,
  Whose hill-tops, crowned with glory,
Rise up 'mong scenes whose names find place
  In dear and deathless story.

WHEN THE SERE LEAFLETS FELL.

Verses to a friend, on receiving intimation of the death of his daughter
at the age of fifteen.

SHE closed her eyes when the sere leaflets fell
O'er the pathway that lies thro' the deep-wooded dell,
Where often her merry voice rang thro' the glade,
When there by the home of her childhood she played.

She faded away when the fairest of flowers
Were swept from the greenwood, the fields, and the bowers,
And Autumn's chill breeze in the dust hath not laid
Aught fairer or purer than that blooming maid.

There are griefs which a brother may help thee to bear,
There are griefs, too, another is helpless to share;
And such 'mid the gloom that o'ershadows your cot;
Yes, such, O bereavëd ones, now is your lot.

Is this, then, the end of that beautiful dream?
Was it closed when she crossed through death's dark rolling
    stream?
Is it yours but to ponder and treasure with tears
The memories strewn over those fifteen brief years?

Ah, no! 'tis not yours to despair or despond;
Hope's rainbow doth stretch to the bright world beyond—
She closëd those beautiful eyes but to wake
Where no fading things on the vision shall break,

Where no flowerets shall fade, where no sere leaves shall fall,
Where Death shall no more spread his dark gloomy pall;
She is safe from all suffering, sorrow, and pain,
Redeemed through the blood of the Lamb that was slain.

All is well, and the dark clouds will soon break away
Invaded by light from the heavenly day;
And what if at last that departed one waits
To welcome you home at the bright pearly gates?
Ah! then, all the grief and the anguish you know
Will be lost in the land where no tears ever flow?

Yet cease not to cherish her memory dear,
Withhold not affection's fond heart-melting tear;
Forbear not to handle, and fondle with care
The raiment, the beautiful ringlet of hair,
That tell of a form, that shall know them no more,
At peace on a brighter and happier shore;
And oft with soft accents her life-story tell,
Whose eyelids were closed when the sere leaflets fell.

FAMILIAR EPISTLE TO MR BEGG,

GRAND-NEPHEW OF ROBERT BURNS.

On receipt of a *fac-simile* of the Kilmarnock Edition of the Poet's Works.

WHEN I received the goodly gift
    Sae lately sent tae me, man,

I ferlied sair if lord or peer
    As vauntie o'er could be, man.
It's honest truth that's in my mouth
    When plainly thee I tell, man,
There is nae ane in a' the lan'
    Wad prize't mair than mysel', man.

I've scann'd it owre an' owre an' owre
    Wi' keen an' eager gaze, man;
An' wi't there cam' a pleasin' gleam
    O' Burns's early days, man,
Ere keen regret his path beset,
    Ere tears had dimmed his e'e, man,
An' care an' strife had rendered life
    A struggle hard tae dree, man.

I've mony a beuk in mony a neuk,
    As ye may well suppose, man;
Works quaint an' queer an' auld an' rare
    Baith poetry an' prose, man;
But frae the best that I can boast
    My fancy aften turns, man,
To wander near the windin' Ayr,
    An' crack wi' Robbie Burns, man.

When neist ye're doon at oor wee toon,
    In valley o' the Lyne, man,
Ye'll spend a twa-three 'oors, I trust,
    At this fireside o' mine, man;
For mair by far than man o' war,
    A throne that overturns, man,
I lo'e the name o' sic as claim
    Kindred wi' Robbie Burns, man.

Then fare-ye-weel, my couthie chiel',
    Until thy face I see, man,
Accept the thanks my tuneless cranks
    Would now convey to thee, man.
An' while the gift sae prized and loved
    Bids me this ditty weave, man,
Be't thine to feel mair blessèd still
    To give than to receive, man.

TO SEPTEMBER.

SEPTEMBER—silent and serene—
  September—sunny, calm and clear—
Thou art the sweetest time I ween,
  To me o' a' the changing year ;
For, when I stray beside the stream,
  Or linger lonely by the lake,
There is no dear departed dream
  Thy gentle touch doth not awake.

Thy sunshine and thy silence breathe
  The names of friends departed long,
Whose smiles shed sunshine o'er my path,
  Whose kindness filled my mouth with song—
Of friends who laid them down to sleep
  In joyous morn of life's young day,
And friends who lived to mourn and weep,
  With tottering form and tresses gray.

The reaper's song brings back to me
  The sunny hairsts o' auld langsyne—
When ban'sters waked the merry lay,
  And maidens fair the lilt did join :
It minds me of the merry throng
  That gathered round the cheerful hearth
To tell the tale and sing the song,
  And pass the hours with jocund mirth.

Yet, oh ! I love to cross the strath
  In this the time of fading flowers,
When lyart leaves lie on the path
  And warblers leave the woodland bowers ;
The sunshine of departing hours,
  The silence of the Autumn day,
And withering leaves and dying flowers
  Have lessons all to heart may lay.

Soon will it fall upon the ear
  The dirge that dull October sings,
Soon will November's blast make bare
  All that in field or forest springs ;

Farewell, then, pensive wanderings,
   When tempests o'er the valley sweep—
And welcome joys that Winter brings,
   'Mid darkness and oblivion deep.

September—silent and serene—
   September—sunny, calm, and clear—
Thou art the sweetest time, I ween,
   To me o' a' the changing year;
For when I stray beside the stream,
   Or linger lonely by the lake,
There is no dear departed dream
   Thy gentle touch doth not awake.

THE GRAVE OF BURNS.

Verses written after a visit to Dumfries.

BACK, 'neath the sultry July sun—
   Back 'neath the Summer's noontide ray,
To scenes for which pure song hath won
   An envied immortality.

Queen of the South! queenly thou art
   In all thy wealth of native grace,
For who that boasts a Scottish heart
   But loves thy beauties all to trace,
Since Scotland's Burns, her sweetest bard,
   Hath found with thee his resting-place.

Yes; we have "roved by bonny Doon,"
   And wandered by the winding Ayr,
Where oft beneath the silver moon
   He breathed his love, his grief, and care,

While brightest fancies still did play
   So freely round his youthful head,
And while life's chequered future lay
   A deep, dark riddle, all unread.

But now we stand by Cluden's Towers,
   And near the Nith we take our way,
Where 'mid the strife of later hours,
   In leisure moments he did stray,

And where the muse of Scotia bound .
   That glorious chaplet round his brow,
Which laughs at Time's destroying hand
   And scorneth every scorner now.

Yes ; we have stood beneath the roof
   Where first the poet saw the light
As from the tempest it emerged
   That fearful January night.

But now 'mid July's sweet perfume,
   Her sunshine bright, and calm repose,
We stand beside the cottage home
   Where that brief pilgrimage did close.

We linger on the threshold now,
   That threshold he had crossed so oft ;
We pace the peaceful dwelling through,
   With bated breath and footfall soft.

Anon the narrow stair we climb,
   And what strange mingled thoughts are nigh
When standing in the very room
   Where Scotland's greatest bard did die !

Fraternal thoughts of Scotland's sons,
   In lands and regions far away,
'Mid double charms that distance lends
   To sights and scenes we now survey,

Bound closely 'mong the memories
   That to his history belong,
Who bade his native land arise,
   Crowned with a diadem of song.

We leave the home revered so much,
   And downward pace the narrow street,
Till, in our wanderings, we reach
   The quaint and ancient churchyard gate,

Where came the crowd of mourners' feet,
   Who bore him to his bed of rest,
When radiant July's sunbeams sweet
   Beheld him laid " low in the dust."

Saint Michael's, ah ! no stranger thou
  On Fame's remote historic page ;
Of Covenanting memories true,
  Thine no ignoble heritage.

But round thee now a light is shed,
  And o'er thee now a ray doth rest,
By which the world for aye shall read—
  "Thrice dear to every Scotsman's breast."

At monarch's feet we have not bowed,
  We 've kissed no earthly sovereign's hand,
But shall we not of this be proud,
  Yea, prouder, that to-day we stand

Where generous Wordsworth smote his breast,
  And mourned for Burns with sorrow true ;
Where Halleck, from the far off West,
  His noblest, proudest raptures knew ;

And where the greatest and the best
  In future years shall still repair,
With kindred spirits of the past
  Mysterious intercourse to share ?

There may be those inclined to ask—
  "Yet wherefore wake thy lowly lyre,
When men more fitted for the task,
  And bards of true poetic fire

Have felt these scenes their souls inspire.
  And breathed in sweet and loving line
Thoughts that no effort could require
  To blot out trifles such as thine ?"

I answer such—Our land is free
  As is the breeze that sweeps along
Our hills, and glens, and streams that he
  Has made the theme of deathless song,

And when I frame my nameless lay
  Beside the Poet's resting-place,
An inward impulse I obey
  That I am powerless to suppress !

THE AULD CLACHAN WORTHIES.

" The short and simple annals of the poor."—Gray.

ANITHER, anither, and still yet anither,
   An' Death lays his cauld an' his merciless hand
On silv'ry-haired sage an' on leal, loving mither,
   Wha ance were the pride and the boast o' the land.
O ! dolefu's the maen heard in mony a dwellin'
   Sin' Winter cam' on wi' his frost an' his snaw ;
The vacant chair tellin' the theme o' our wailin'—
   The Auld Clachan worthies are wearin' awa.'

I whiles sit me' doon, i' the cauld Winter's gloamin',
   To think on the hames that langsyne I weel kent,
Where licht hearts were leapin' an' bricht een were beamin,'
   An' true worth did flourish where wealth was ne'er kent,
Where kind faithfu' sons did the parents' lives brichten,
   An' dochters as pure as the new driven snaw ;
Though siccan blithe scenes noo mair rarely we licht on—
   The Auld Clachan worthies are wearin' awa'.

I like aye to muse on the laigh theekit sheelin',
   Wi' divot-built riggin' an' raips roun' the lum ;
The but an' the ben o' the humble Scotch hallan ;
   The hearty Scotch welcome for a' that may come ;
The bricht e'enin' fire, to the rauntle-tree bleezin',
   That lit up the cottage, clean, cosie, an' a',
Where Time's speedy flicht, amang scenes sae enticin',
   Was mark'd by the queer wudden wag-at-the-wa'.

At kirk, when I join in the prayers an' the praises,
   I canna help thinkin'—e'en if it's a sin—
On sairly booed bodies, an' kindly auld faces,
   That now if I look for 'tis only in vain.
The stieve-hamilt staff an' the plain shepherd's plaidie
   Are sichts by whilk rarely oor path noo is crossed,
Tho' oft hae they graced, at kirk, fair, mill, and smiddy,
   As kind sons as e'er Mither Scotland could boast.

In days when ae change chases hard on anither,
   We whiles maun thole changes no juist for the best ;
When bald-headed carle an' reverend faither
   Maun bow to the wisdom by striplings possessed.

An' doesna dissemblance aft eagerly gather
　Fruits that should to truth, worth, an' honesty fa' ?
We 're a' tapsalteerie, we 're a' wrang thegither—
　The Auld Clachan worthies are wearin' awa'.

They 're wearin' awa', an' wi' them too we 're tynin'
　The beauty an' grace o' oor auld mither tongue,
That aft round oor young hearts gaed witchingly twinin'
　In tales, sangs, an' ballads, they tauld an' they sung.
There 'll sune be nocht left to remind 's o' them, savin'
　The auld sculptured-through stanes richt near the kirk wa',
That silently tell, where the rank grass is wavin'—
　The Auld Clachan worthies are wearin' awa'.

THIS FAIRY GLEN.

UNKNOWN to the pages of wonderful story,
　Unknown to the minstrel's sweet soul-stirring lay ;
Yet clothed with a beauty and crowned with a glory
　Which poet or artist can never pourtray,
Thro' many fair scenes in the past I 've been guided.
　But none half so fair have I gazed upon yet ;
And many dear dreams from my mem'ry have faded,
　But this Fairy Glen I can never forget.

Bright streamlet ! since last on thy banks I was seated,
　I 've battled the changes of many long years ;
Prosperity's sunbeams I often have greeted,
　Nor have I been stranger to Misery's tears ;
And yet 'mid the changes within and around me,
　The sun of my love for this scene ne'er hath set,
So closely thy mem'ries have wrapt, yea, have bound me,
　That this Fairy Glen I can never forget.

Unlike the scenes pictured in youth's golden vision
　Are those among which my life's lot hath been cast ;
Yet blest with leal hearts that around me have risen,
　Kind sons and fair daughters so dear to my breast ;
No cause for complaining, no room for repining,
　No home has my bosom for idle regret,
Yet thoughts of past pleasure are still a sweet treasure,
　And this Fairy Glen I can never forget.

WE ARE NOT GROWING OLD.

"All men think all men mortal but themselves."—Young.

WE are not growing old, oh no! How foolish thus to speak,
Tho' wrinkles now may cross the brow, and furrows plough
    the cheek ;
A very idle story this, a tale so often told,
We do not care such words to hear,—We are not growing
    old.

We are not growing old, tho' gallant sons around us rise,
And daughters fair, with all the love in woman's breast that
    lies ;
The thought of age can only grow in climate chill and cold,
Not 'mid the mirth that cheers our hearth,—We are not
    growing old.

We are not growing old, tho' oft, with eyes bedimmed with
    tears,
We scan the chequered history, of well nigh forty years ;
But ah, more eagerly we turn to what remains untold,
And on the future build our hopes,—We are not growing
    old.

We are not growing old, although our locks are mixed with
    grey,
And baldness overtake us, these are no criterion ; nay,
How often do we meet with such in manhood strong and bold ;
Decisive proof they do not give,—We are not growing old.

We are not growing old ; let such a thought be far away,
We yet perchance may meet it on some very distant day ;
But even when threescore and ten may o'er our heads
    have roll'd,
Ah, still I fear we 'll think, even then,—We are not growing
    old.

We are not growing old, oh no. How foolish thus to speak,
Tho' wrinkles now may cross the brow, and furrows plough
    the cheek ;
A very idle story this, a tale so often told,
We do not care such words to hear, We are not growing old.

MY RICHES.

My riches are my little ones,
  No other wealth I claim
Save these, my merry romping sons,
  My daughters dear by name.
And though unheeded be my lot,
  My destiny obscure,
With peace and comfort in my cot,
  You may not call me poor.

My riches are my little ones,
  With lusty shouts who come
Across the room to welcome me
  When evening brings me home,
Whose winsome smiles shed sunshine on
  Life's weary chequered way;
And in my times of sadness chase
  All grief and care away.

My riches are my little ones,
  Who nightly with me raise,
To Him who gives us every good,
  The humble hymn of praise;
The tender plants whose constant care
  Hath unto me been given,
Whose little lips I taught to say
  "Father, who art in heaven."

My riches are my little ones:
  O! think not I despise
The beauty of those rosy cheeks,
  Those heaven-lit soft blue eyes!—
Those ruby lips, those rounded arms,
  Those locks of curling gold,
More precious are than wide domains
  Whose acres are untold.

A CHRISTMAS AND NEW YEAR'S GREETING
TO A
RESIDENT IN KINCARDINE-ON-FORTH.

TEN words to thee, dear brither ———,
Noo pairted frae thy native toon,
An' steerin' duly to the North,
Art ling'rin' on the banks o' Forth,
Thir twa three lines that noo I'm writin'
Will prove ye arena quite forgotten.
But in this time o' happy meetin's,
O' Guid New Years, and kindly greetin's,
That face and form afore us rise,
Free frae dissemblance an' disguise,
And, listening wi' a fond impatience,
We hear ance mair yer strange orations,
Or gar ance mair the rafter ring
Owre jokes ye pass an' sangs ye sing,
For aften hae ye held them laughin',
The worthies o' oor ain auld clachan ;
Though a' yer jokes, turned inside out,
Were free o' guile beyond a doubt.

While cosily I'm seated here
Beside the ingle bleezin' clear,
I've pored an' read twa hours an' mair,
Till type's grown dim, an' een grown sair,
An' now till midnight hour shall clink,
I wish to sit an' think an' think.
The past I'll strive to conjure up,
An' keek through the kaleidoscope
At chequer'd scenes o' guid an' ill,
When joy or grief the breast did thrill,
Our aims an' hopes, our cares an' crosses,
Our frequent gains, mair frequent losses,
Our times when hand unseen has led us,
An' times when guidance seemed denied us,
An' for our future conduct draw
Some lessons worthy o' them a'.

E

'Tis Christmas Eve while here I sit,
An' at this hour what myriads wait
To welcome in the blessed morn
On which the Prince of Peace was born.
Had we been nurtured south the Tweed,
In this we twa wad been agreed
To join the sweet and holy hymn
In church or chapel lighted dim.
But reared on Scotland's rugged coast,
Where Knox and Calvin rule the roast,
Auld-warld Puritanic pride
Sic wholesome pleasure has denied,
And when sic sacred seasons come,
Submissively we a' sit dumb.
Be that's it may, peace be wi' them
Devoutly who observe the same,
To all the faithful joy be given
In every nation under heaven.
I speak to ane wha like mysel'
Likes weel the deep and wooded dell,
Where wind the waters o' the Lyne,
'Mong scenes sae dear sin' auld langsyne;
Wha likes to name ilk bonnie brae
We climbed in youth's delightful day,
And asked, with proud exultant air,
What spot in a' the warld sae fair?

But vainly on sic themes we speak,
When Winter winds blaw cauld an' bleak,
Let's wait till Spring's sweet sunshine come
To bid the flow'rets bud an' bloom;
Till we ance mair the primrose see,
An' daisies on the dappled lea,
When we may hear the warbler's strain
Re-echoing through the woods again;
An' mid ilk pleasin' sicht an' sound
We'll share the joy that reigns around,
An' seek ance mair the sweet repose
That reigns where bright West Water flows,
Or tread the dells we lo'e sae dearly,
Where limpid Lyne meanders clearly.

Or breathe the clear and halesome air
On peacefu' Leadlaw's uplands fair,
Or hear the saftly sighin' gale
Through Medwyn Dell, around Lynedale,
Or feel o' joy the liveliest thrill,
When ling'rin' by the auld Lint Mill.

But wherefore thus prolong this screed
To sermon length, that nane may read ?
I only meant to wish ye here
A hearty an' a guid New Year,
Wi' peace an' plenty, free frae care
Through changes o' richt mony a year.
An' now attend to my instruction,
Convey my faithful benediction
To freends an' cronies ane an' a',
Wha did sae muckle kindness shaw,
When in the lang, lang days o' June
I visited yer ancient toon.
(Their names I needna try to gie—
Ye ken them better far than me.)
How wonderfu' to think since then
Sax months an' mair hae come an' gane;
Let 's hope the time is drawing nigh—
Say when the neist sax hae gane by— .
That I my footsteps may retrace
To many a dear and sacred place ;
For I could weel repeat an hour
At Culross on yon ancient tower ;
Or gazing on yon sculpture rare
Within the peaceful house of prayer ;
Or wand'rin' 'mang the kirkyard trees
That nod to every passing breeze,
O'er tombstones sculptured rude and rough,
Where text and telling epitaph
Beseech the passer-by to know
How very brief's his life below;
Or when the Sabbath's silence reigns,
Survey the peaceful wide spread plains,
Or join the simple psalm again
In yonder stately sacred fane ;

Or scale aince mair yon sunny height
To gaze with fresh and keen delight
On distant scenes and sights that tell us
Of Bruce and glorious William Wallace.

Oh brither Scots! who still retain
The patriot's blood fresh in the vein,
When ye your country's honour toast,
And of her rugged beauty boast,
Shall we forget to honour them
Wha earned her freedom with their fame ?

But lest by this renewed digression
I 'm owre the bounds o' a' discretion,
I 'll drap my pen, my task I 'll end ;
Trusting you 'll pardon a' that 's penned
By ane on wham ye can depend,
A trusty, true, an' faithfu' friend.

OOR AULD STRATHSPEYS AN' REELS.

Gae bring my lo'esome fiddle ben, let 's hae a rantin' tune :
I haena drawn a bow d'ye ken, sin' last we saw the moon.
The gloamin' never seems sae glum, the nicht ne'er looks sae lang,
As when oor cozie cottage hame kens neither tune nor sang.

Wi' "Tullochgorm," "Monymusk," an "Delvinside" sae rare,
Wi' "Speed the plough," "Kilravock's reel," an' "Merry lads o' Ayr,"
We 'll wake anew the genial thrill that thro' the bosom steals,
When listnin' to their lichtsome lilt, "Oor auld Strathspeys and reels."

What tho' "the snaws are drifted deep," owre wold, an' glen, an' lea,
An' fierce an' furious tempests sweep oot-owre baith land an' sea !
But little o' the Winter's wrath in oor wee cot we ken,
An' cauld John Frost maun be dismissed frae oor wee but-an'-ben.

We'll gar them ring wi' mony a spring frae Fraser and
    Neil Gow,
Frae Marshall too an' mony mae brave champions o' the
    bow;
An deep's the debt auld Scotland owes to leal true-hearted
    chiels
Wha siccan legacy bequeathed—"Oor Auld Strathspeys and
    Reels."

Let others praise the lifeless lays frae distant lands we hear,
Frae Switzerland or Germany—awa' wi' a' sic gear;
To join the dance wi' sons o' France, or wi' her daughters
    braw,
Is e'en a thocht that frae this breast is unco far awa'.

Then let me hear the clarion clear; or bagpipe wild an'
    shrill
In distant dell or woody glen, or on the heath-clad hill;
Yet liveliest is the thrill that thro' the inmost bosom steals
When lichtsomely the fiddle lilts "Oor Auld Strathspeys
    and Reels."

YET ANOTHER.

Thoughts suggested by the Fall of the Leaf.

YET another! yet another! Autumn's sapless leaves and sere
From their branches fall and flutter, telling tales of Winter
    near—
Soon no trace of Summer's foliage in the wildwood will
    remain,
And November will wail sadly through a desolate domain.

Yet another! yet another! so they fade—so pass away,
Playmates of our sunny childhood, friends of youth's delight-
    ful day;
And we love to ponder o'er them, though our eyes be dim-
    med with tears,
Who made light the joyous sunshine of our youth's unsullied
    years.

Yet another! yet another! so they pass those years of ours—
Spring with its delightful sunshine, Summer with its songs
    and flowers,
Autumn with its golden treasures, Winter with its angry
    blast—
Pointing forward to the latest, leading onward to the last.

Yet another! yet another! Autumn's sapless leaves and sere
Fall and flutter from their branches, telling tales of Winter
    near—
Soon no trace of Summer's foliage in the wildwood will
    remain,
And November will wail sadly through a desolate domain.

HER VOICE ALONE REMAINED THE SAME.

HER voice alone remained the same;
    All else seemed changed, and sadly too:
Those lips did not so rosy seem,
    Nor yet so bright those eyes of blue;
And on that once fair, placid brow,
    Where peace and joy their watch did keep,
Grim care had yoked her ruthless plough,
    And driven furrows long and deep.

Her voice alone remained the same—
    Though since I last its tones had heard,
It oft had fanned love's purest flame
    By many a sweet and soothing word;
O! happy they who have been reared,
    And happy they who have been trained,
'Mid sunshine of a life so pure,
    And fondness of a heart so kind.

Her voice alone remained the same;
    That voice which oft her love had told
When straying by the mountain stream,
    Or wandering o'er the Autumn wold;
And yet to think that love waxed cold—
    And what gave pleasure now gives pain;
Nor wealth, nor power, nor lands, nor gold,
    Could ever bridge that breach again.

Her voice alone remained the same ;
   Yet it seemed meet it should be so,
For back with it the vision came
   Of youth's bright years and "Long ago,"
And many a bitter tear did flow ;
   Yet tears they were brought no relief—
They came from founts that overflow
   With hidden and unspoken grief.

Her voice alone remained the same ;
   O that it never more may hear
Sounds sweet mid youth's unclouded dream
   But now so painful to the ear !
It seems as if I wandered near
   Some hallowed spot with ruthless tread,
Or sacriligeously laid bare
   The ashes of the much-loved dead.

KIRKCUDBRIGHT.

Verses to an old Schoolmate in the Parish of Dalry, after frequent invitations to visit him, and spend a few days in the district.

DECEMBER thirty-first's the date ;
Yes, an' the nicht is waxin' late,
The year's last hours noo to the gaet
      Glide speedily—
Thae hours I gladly dedicate,
      Dear friend, to thee.

The year that's noo sae near a close
Richt mony an unsolved problem shows,
An' mony an unread riddle knows—
      We'll no conceal't—
What's waur, richt mony a vow, alas !
      Left unfulfill't.

Of keen remorse I feel the touch—
The inward sting of self-reproach;
The kindness shown to me sae much
      I brawly ken,
Beyond what I could ever reach
      My fellow-men.

Yet cauld an' careless tho' I seem,
Ye maunna for a moment dream
That I ignore the richtfu' claim
       Friendship wad raise,
For ane wha shared wi' me the dream
       O' life's young days.

The thocht my inmost bosom cheers,
That we 'll rehearse the joys and fears
O' muckle mair than thretty years,
       An' crousely craw
That still the bark in safety steers;
       Nor is that a'—

To bosoms Scottish to the core
There 's mony a sight an' scene in store,
That we wi' pleasure may explore
       An' true delight,
Where Criffel's brow or Solway shore
       Break on the sight.

There 's mony a bonny auld kirkyard
Retains aneath its rankling sward
The dust o' men to death that dared
       Still to be true;
Wha's mem'ries we may weel regard
       Wi' reverence due.

There 's mony a wild romantic glen,
By crystal Cree an' lonely Ken,
Made sacred by the Covenant men
       O' bygone days,
Whose histories a halo len'
       Nought can erase.

An' thinkna ye I 'd like to hear
The murmurin' o' the streamlets clear,
That did wi' voice o' praise an' prayer
       Mingle an' join,
When faithfu' men did fealty swear
       Or Covenants sign ?

An' thinkna ye I'd like to tread
The lonely moorlands where they're laid,
The noble, tho' the nameless, dead,
  That scattered lie;
For Scotland's weal who fought an' bled
  Wi' purpose high?

O, Scotia! our dear native land!
There's no a nook on a' thy strand
But has its legends, rich an' grand,
  Stirrin' an' rare,
To them wha hae thy history scanned
  E'en wi'-sma' care.

It's no when Janwar winds are high,
When deep her snaw-wreaths round us lie,
That I, howe'er, will seek Dalry;
  We'll choose our day
In lightsome June, leafy July,
  Or rosy May.

Sae, till the daisies deck the sod,
Glenkin's lone wilds shall be allowed
In solitude to lie untrod
  By feet o' mine;
Yet then I'll seek my friend's abode
  For auld langsyne.

December thirty-first, still later—
I drap my pen, an' close my letter,
An' though it's but a rhymin' clatter
  That here I send,
If now I feel I'm less yere debtor
  I've gained my end.

THE END OF A LONELY LIFE.

Suggested by a November funeral scene. Died, November, 188—;
aged 84.

"FOUR score and four;" such was the tale that coffin lid
 did tell
Of one whom all the villagers had known so long and well:

It came, the end of that long life of sorrow, grief, and care,
"When chill November's surly blast made fields an' forests
    bare."
His heritage had been for long "a desolated hearth,"
Where hushed for ever was the song of youthful, joyous
    mirth;
The partner of his early years had crossed the Jordan's
    flood—
Cut down while in the noon of life, in prime of woman-
    hood;
A dire consumption swept away the daughters of his love;
An only son, who promis'd fair his comforter to prove,
He, too, did meekly bow the head when heart and flesh
    gave way—
He, too, did say "Thy will be done," when came the awful
    day.
Yet in and out the old man went beneath the dark eclipse,
While, Aaron-like, he held his peace, no murmur on his lips.

At last it came; an end of peace; may we such comfort
    share,
What matter, then, tho' wildest blasts make fields and forests
    bare.
We stood beside his dying bed; few loving friends were
    there
To wipe away the cold death sweat and bless the poor man's
    bier;
And as we sadly pondered o'er life's solemn mysteries,
Back came the faces and the forms of those that once were
    his;
And oft we asked while ling'ring 'mid the silence of that
    room—
Are holy angels hovering near to guide the pilgrim home,
To those that dwell in that fair land, unknown to grief or
    care,
Where no November's surly blast makes fields and forests
    bare?

We saw the pilgrim laid to rest, the mourners were but few,
For wealth can purchase many things, yea, purchase mourners
    too;

It mattered not, with him 'twas past, and as we homeward
    turned,
A strange and pleasant flame anew within the bosom burned
Of gratitude to him who waked the tender wail of woe,
When he did tread our Scottish soil a hundred years ago—
In deathless lays who sung the Doon, the Afton, and the
    Ayr,
"When chill November's surly blast made fields an' forests
    bare."

THE BLOSSOMS IN HER HAIR.

In a somewhat bleak and lonely spot, near the junction of the parishes
of Linton and Pennicuik, and at a considerable height above the bed of
the North Esk, but in its immediate neighbourhood, is the Loch of Marfield, a favourite resort in winter of the lovers of the roaring game.   This
pool of water has, within the remembrance of many persons still living,
been the scene of many a tragic occurrence.   The last was the death of an
amiable young woman who was a servant in the farm house of Marfield.
One summer day she was attending to field work as usual, tedding
hay and singing some of her favourite songs.   On the afternoon she was
driving some cows to a field adjoining the Loch, and, passing the garden,
she leaned over the fence, plucked a portion of rowan tree blossom, put
it hastily in her hair, and hastened in the direction of the Loch.   Her
absence caused alarm, and, a few hours afterwards her lifeless body was
discovered lying in the loch, the rowan tree blossom still entangled in her
hair.   The following was written after visiting the spot.

GLOOMY lake, my heart grows eerie
    'Mong these moorlands bleak and dreary,
As I gaze upon thy waters, sullen, motionless, and low ;
    O'er thy chamber, dark and narrow,
    Hovers many a tale of sorrow ;
But the shadow waxes deeper with this tale of weird and
    woe.

'Twas not trembling age that found thee
    With night's sable darkness round thee,
Nor the hopeless maniac, raving 'mid the anguish of despair ;
    But a maiden—in life's morning,
    With bright wreaths her brow adorning—
Who went down into the waters with the blossoms in her
    hair.

When the noonday sun was beaming,
Bright her youthful eye was gleaming,
And her wonted songs were wafted on the balmy summer's air,
But ere evening's peaceful shadows
Gathered o'er the moors and meadows,
She was slumbering 'mong the waters with the blossoms in
her hair.

Say not, think not there was nothing
Which that youthful heart was writhing;
Ah, the dreadful day of judgment many mysteries will declare,
And the dawning of that morrow
Shall lay bare her secret sorrow,
Who went down into the waters with the blossoms in her hair.

Of thy grief, fond, faithful father,
Of thy anguish, loving mother,
Tho' we ponder oft in silence, yet to speak we will not dare;
Words seem foolish, rash, forbidden,
O'er a grief so great and hidden,
As was thine o'er her who perished with the blossoms in her
hair.

Mourn, ye nymphs, and swains, oh mourn her—
Think what anguish must have torn her,
Ere she bowed her head to enter the dark portals of despair;
Sad the tale now oft repeated,
By the glowing hearth while seated,
Of the maiden who did perish with the blossoms in her hair.

Yet, let silence ne'er be broken
By one word unkindly spoken,
O'er the sad untimely fate of one so winsome, young, and fair.
Think on hearts, now heavy-laden,
That shall life-long mourn the maiden
Who went down into the waters with the blossoms in her hair.

Gloomy lake, I haste to leave thee,
While this mournful dirge I weave thee.
Evening shadows swiftly gather o'er the moorlands bleak
Thoughts of gloom and sadness only,   [and bare;
Haunt this spot so bleak and lonely,
Where we mourn the youthful maiden with the blossoms in
her hair.

ONE DAUGHTER.

ONE daughter, yes, and only one,
  Amid the merry throng
That nestle round the cheerful hearth,
  When nights are cold and long;
That make the lighted room resound
  With many a pleasant hymn,
And 'mid their frolics often lisp
  Mother's and father's name.

One daughter, yes, and only one,
  She romps around me now,
With health upon her rosy cheek,
  And sunshine on her brow;
With flaxen locks profusely curled,
  So beautiful and fair,
And bright blue eyes; oh! what a world
  Of merriment is there.

One daughter, yes, and only one,
  And round that playful thing
Her loving brothers, one and all,
  With fond affection cling.
Her little wants, her tiny cares,
  Their constant thoughts employ;
She is the centre, and the sun,
  Of all their simple joy.

One daughter, yes, and only one,
  And o'er her future lot
This bosom often feels the thrill
  Of many an anxious thought.
Yet, wherefore, with untimely care,
  Should I becloud my brow?
Let me be faithful to my flock,
  And happy 'mong them now.

One daughter, yes, and only one,
  No other e'er was ours;
Death yet hath passed our humble home,
  And spared our little flowers.

And oft when graver moments come,
  And times of holier thought,
I tremble when I think I am
  Not grateful as I ought.

THE RINGLET OF HAIR.

" The lock of hair shown you by my brother has been preserved in our family for several generations. My late father was the last who could tell anything of its history, but so long is it since he spoke of it to my brother that the facts have escaped his remembrance, and since the death of my father the whole is wrapt in mystery."—Extract from a letter by an old school-fellow.

It was a rich ringlet of golden hair
  In a secret spot which lay ;
A memory bright of a radiant light
  Which had long since passed away.
Yea, the hearts were hushed which o'er it did
  With fond affection swell,
And the latest lips by death were sealed
  Which its mystic tale could tell.

It was a rich ringlet of golden hair
  Had been carefully treasured and long,
For sire to son had handed it down,
  The holiest relics among.
And in accents brief its tale was told,
  And in tones suppressed and low,
But all about that lock of gold
  Is the darkest mystery now.

It was a rich ringlet of golden hair,
  Perhaps of some cherub child
Which had lent to the dwelling a heavenly air
  And gladdened whene'er it smiled.
But o'er its path the shadow of death
  Did fall in the morn of day,
And its name is enrolled in the numerous fold
  Of the early called away.

It was a rich ringlet of golden hair :
  Yes, and perchance it may
Have braided the brow of some maiden fair
  In her youth's delightful day ;
Some virgin pure, with snow-white brow,
  And voice of silvery sound,
Whose bridal bed had been early made
  In the churchyard's lonely mound.

It was a rich ringlet of golden hair,
  And thro' many a changing year
May fond hearts cherish with faithful care
  What was to their loved ones dear ;
And strange emotions yet untold
  Shall to life in the bosom spring,
As their fingers unfold that ringlet of gold—
  That prized and precious thing.

It was a rich ringlet of golden hair,
  In a secret spot which lay ;
A memory bright of a radiant light
  Which had long since passed away.
Yea, the hearts were hushed that o'er it did
  With fond affection swell,
And the latest lips by death were sealed
  Which its mystic tale could tell.

RAVENDEAN BURN.*

RAVENDEAN BURN ! Ravendean Burn !
  Wimpling and dimpling the blue hills among ;
Health on the breeze of the valley is borne
  Where 'mong the mountains is heard thy sweet song.
Far from the haunts and the dwellings of men,
  Far from green meadow and daisied lea,
Singing where silence and solitude reign,
  Sweet are the moments spent musing by thee.

*A small mountain stream, rising near the Wolf Crags, on the north-west boundry of Peeblesshire, where, according to tradition, Conventicles were held in the days of the persecution.

Ravendean Burn! Ravendean Burn!
  Rude tho' thy ravings in Winter days be,
When woods by the breath of the tempest are torn,
  And Winter winds wail o'er the daisyless lea,
Still there is music—majestic and grand—
  In thy rude torrent's rush, heard from afar,
In days when the storm sweeps ocean and land,
  Thro' nights all unknown unto moonbeam or star.

Ravendean Burn! Ravendean Burn!
  Say, on thy banks did our forefathers meet,
When Zion's fair banner was ruthlessly torn
  By tyrants who trampled it under their feet?
Ah! ne'er did the sweet voice of prayer and praise
  Arise among wilds more befitting, I ween,
And ne'er, 'mid the troubles of Covenant days,
  Was the preacher's voice heard in a lonelier scene.

Ravendean Burn! Ravendean Burn!
  Wimpling and dimpling the blue hills among;
Health on the breeze of the valley is borne
  Where 'mong the mountains is heard thy sweet song.
Far from the haunts and the dwellings of men,
  Far from green meadow and daisied lea, .
Singing where silence and solitude reign,
  Sweet are the moments spent musing by thee.

NOONDAY DARKNESS.

Verses written on the sudden darkness with which our land was visited
on 12th August, 1884, a day rendered memorable to many by the sudden
death of the Earl of Lauderdale.

OH! day to be remembered!
  Full many a tongue shall tell
Of the mysterious darkness
  That at the noontide fell,
When thrice ten thousand bosoms
  Were wrung with bitter fear
Lest the last dread tribunal
  Were near, aye, very near.

NOONDAY DARKNESS.

It was a dreadful darkness,
  And swiftly did it fall;
For oh! the Hand was powerful
  That spread the gloomy pall;
And mighty was the Monarch
  Who shrouded in dismay
The work of His creation—
  The creatures of a day.

A weird and awful silence
  Did for an instant reign,
That moment one of anguish,
  Of keen and poignant pain,
Ere yet the agonising
  And terrible suspense
Was closed amid the thund'rings
  Of dread Omnipotence.

It was a dreadful darkness,
  And brief altho' it was,
Earth's thoughtless sons waxed thoughtful,
  Earth's hasty sons did pause;
And the persistent scoffer
  Has through new troubles passed,
And doubts if all his doubting
  Will bear him up at last.

It was a dreadful darkness,
  And musing on the same,
Backward our thoughts are turned
  To One of gracious name,
The tidings of whose anguish
  And sweat, and pain, and tears
Have reached us through the changes
  Of thrice six hundred years.

It was a solemn picture,
  Such as perchance no more
Will meet us till the myst'ries
  Of this brief life are o'er,

When He who cried, 'Tis finished,
 'Mid noonday darkness shall
Appear in awful glory—
 The Lord and Judge of all.

Oh! day to be remembered,
 Full many a tongue shall tell
Of the mysterious darkness
 That at the noon-tide fell,
When thrice ten thousand bosoms
 Were wrung with bitter fear
Lest the last dread tribunal
 Were near, aye, very near.

I WINNA LEAVE AULD SCOTLAND YET.

I WINNA leave auld Scotland yet,
 Though tryin' times we 're doomed to dree,
An' mony a brither seeks a hame
 Far owre the wide Atlantic Sea.
Success to many a manly band,
 Who hardship, storm, and danger brave!
But in our ain dear mountain land
 I wish at last to find a grave.

I winna leave auld Scotland yet—
 Dear are her glens and wooded dales,
Her moors, where owre the martyr's bed
 The Summer wind sae saftly wails;
Her crystal streams, that gladly glide
 The green majestic hills among;
Her rivers, that have long been wed
 To soothing, sweet, undying song.

I winna leave auld Scotland yet—
 A better future is in store,
When sunshine bright the scene shall light
 That sorrow long has hovered o'er.
Then Scotchmen on their native shore,
 And brethren on a distant strand,
Shall join in glad rejoicings o'er
 Our ancient Covenanted land.

I winna leave auld Scotland yet,
  Though tryin' times we're doomed to dree,
An' mony a brither seeks a hame
  Far owre the wide Atlantic Sea.
Success to many a manly band
  Who hardship, storm, and danger brave!
But in our ain dear mountain land
  I wish at last to find a grave

PARTING TRIBUTE.

To the Rev. William Whitefield, Author of Various Sketches of the
Covenanters, &c., on his departure for America.

AND dost thou leave thy native land when dark December
    reigns,
To sojourn on a foreign strand, and seek, on distant plains,
A home from Scotland's battlefields so very far removed,
From hills and streams renowned in song, by thee so fondly
    loved?

And will thy bosom be at rest when thou no more shalt tread
The wilds and misty moors to which the faithful often fled?
When thou no more shalt look upon the lonely martyr's hill,
Or glens by Cameron made dear, or Peden, or Cargill?

Then it can only be thou art to kindred spirits joined,
That know and share thy love to all that thou dost leave
    behind,
By whom the patriotic flame to life anew is fanned,
Of love to Mother Scotland's name, our ancient Covenant land.

Thus may it be, and Scotland still shall have the fruits that
    flow
From early years spent 'mong her hills, that holiest memories
    know;
While bravest deeds of daring, noblest acts of godly men,
Find full and faithful record thro' thy person and thy pen.

SUGGESTED BY "REMINISCENCES OF YARROW,"
BY THE LATE DR JAMES RUSSELL.

A GENIAL sunbeam serenely reflected
    By sire deeply skilled in the Borderland lore ;
The past with its lights and shadows depicted
    By hand that shall now lift the pencil no more.

And dear to the daughters and sons of the Forest
    The tales of their valley so classic and fair,
Recorded by one of the truest and purest
    That e'er trod its mountains or breathed its air,

Who oft sought their homes in the dark hours of sorrow.
    With kind words of comfort the downcast to raise,
Who learned, 'mid the brightest rejoicings in Yarrow,
    No face and no form was more welcome than his.

No bigoted cleric, no narrow sectarian,
    Pursuant of honour, promotion, or fame—
The plain simple pastor, and faithful historian,
    A Scot, and a Border-man worthy the name ;

Who loved Yarrow fondly in life's joyous morning,
    When bright golden dreams did his fancy engage;
Yet loved her still more when gray tresses gave warning
    Of life's closing scenes and the frailties of age.

Now Yarrow's green hills greet the sunbeams as freely,
    And Yarrow's lone waves their sad songs do not cease ;
Tho' softest their murm'rings in depth of the valley
    Where pastor and people are resting in peace.

A genial sunbeam serenely reflected
    By sire deeply skilled in the Borderland lore;
The past with its lights and its shadows depicted
    By hand that shall now lift the pencil no more.

MR PETER DUNLOP, ANTIQUARIAN, MILLBURN.

LANGSYNE noo a cleric, queer ane,
  Sang in sweet an' stirring strains
O' that generous antiquarian—
  Adam Sim, o' Coulter Mains.

Now, a plain, unlettered layman,
  Seeks in simple terms to tell,
O' the young aspiring claimant
  Upon whom his mantle fell.

Orthodox in style and metre,
  Modestly we would applaud him;
And, although his name be "Peter,"
  Isna that as guid as Adam?

True, his was a lofty dwellin',
  Costin' thousands aught or ten;
Peter's is a hamely hallan—
  Just a Scottish but-an'-ben.

Yet aneath that roof sae humble
  Gathered noo's a store, I ween,
That successfully micht jumble
  Ony head but Peter's ain.

How sae mony auld and rare things
  Into his possession fell,
Is anither o' the queer things
  He can best explain himsel'.

Tools and weapons, representing
  Times of peace and times of war;
Some frae weel-kent cave or mountain,
  Some frae countries distant far;

Some frae lone hilltap that rises,
  Reaching maist unto the moon;
Ithers dug frae bogs and mosses,
  Feet—ay, yards—ay, fathoms doon!

Some o' them could claim a hist'ry
  An' a glorious pedigree;
Some o' them are wrapt in mystery
  Dark as dungeon's gloom could be.

Let a friend, then, true an' trusty,
　Celebrate his name in metre—
North and South and East and West hae
　Poured their treasures in to Peter.

Then for coins! a world o' wonders
　Liveliest admiration claim,
Not by scores nor yet by hunders,
　But by thousands counts he them.

'Mong them ye may walc an' grovel
　Through a summer's afternoon;
Some are oblong, ithers oval,
　Some triangular, some roun'.

Some there are wha's clear inscription
　Tell their country an' their age,
Others baffle a' description
　O' philosopher an' sage.

'Mang them, too, there is a sprinklin',
　Coined—I trust I am na wrang—
Ere the stars were set a twinklin',
　Or the moon kent whaur to gang!

Wonder, then, nae man, that men o'
　Wisdom sound, an' common-sense
Hae contracted the vile sin o'
　Lustin' after "Peter's Pence."

Willie Shakespeare says—"There is a
　Tide in the affairs of men;"
May the tidal wave increase aye
　Peter's store baith but an' ben.

May the streamlet turn a river—
　Ane that isna easy cross'd;
And may fortune still thee favour,
　As she has throughout the past.

And, when next I seek the valleys
　O' thy ain dear native shire,
Where still lives the name of Wallace,
　Guarded as with sword of fire;

When I climb each well-known mountain,
  Seek each river, lake, an' stream;
Gaze upon each crystal fountain,
  Dear 'mid youth's delightful dream,

Thoughts, owre pleasant for revealin',
  Shall within this bosom burn
When I seek thy humble shielin',
  Sage an' prophet o' Millburn.

May I find thee snugly seated,
  Isaac's specs upon thy nose,
Abraham's auld sandals fitted
  On the tap of o' Terah's hose.

Quaint and queer remarks to offer
  On this relic and on that;
Garron nails, or splints o' Gophar
  Frae the tap o' Ararat.

Or the harp that David played on
  To the crusty, cross King Saul,
Who got up and threw his javelin
  At his head, but struck the wall.

Weel for us that David watched him,
  And took heels to save his head;
Had that cranky weapon reached him
  We had haen few psalms to read.

But, lest sacred things should suffer
  Frae my touch by tongue or pen,
Friendship's hand I 'd better offer—
  Sae, farewell; amen, amen!

———

ALL ALONE.

You 'll leave me all alone to-night
  Amid the silence of my room;
I cannot wish that others might
  Be sharers in this hour of gloom.

So till the light again has come,
  And clouds and shadows all are gone,
Of my desires this is the sum—
  You'll kindly leave me all alone.

You'll leave me all alone to-night—
  A host of memories are near,
From bygone years they've winged their flight,
  And hover closely round me here.
Faces and forms once very dear—
  How dear none other e'er can know;
So when they claim a sigh, a tear,
  I cannot, dare not, bid them go.

You'll leave me all alone to-night,
  Nor deem me cruel or unkind;
For though my present is made bright
  By smiles of many a loving friend,
Yet bygone loves and friendships lend
  To present times their tinge and hue;
Let me have, then, this hour to spend,
  Those loves and friendships to renew.

You'll leave me all alone to-night
  Amid the silence of my room;
I cannot wish that others might
  Be sharers in this hour of gloom.
So till the light again has come,
  And clouds and shadows all are gone,
Of my desires this is the sum—
  You'll kindly leave me all alone.

FALLEN AND FALLING LEAVES.
Suggested by an October scene.

THEY fall with every fitful breeze,
  They pass away like passing thought—
Nurslings of April and of May
  That July to perfection brought.
They thickly strew the greenwood glade,
  Or flutter o'er the dark blue pool,
Ten thousand leaves that lately made
  The forest scene so beautiful.

Whilst some abruptly quit the stem
   And hasten to earth's bosom cold,
Yet others, all unlike to them,
   Reluctant, quit their fragile hold ;
Whilst some to peaceful rest descend
   'Mong scenes they once did beautify,
And others, all unlike to them,
   Along the wold unheeded lie.

And these have draped the woodland scene
   Where warblers waked their sweetest song,
And those the glen and bowers, I ween,
   Where lovers met and lingered long ;
And these have graced the hedgerows green
   Where sported oft the playful child,
And those the lonely moorland scene
   Where streamlets stray in deserts wild.

Is there no language whispered us
   When wand'ring thro' the leafless woods ?
Ah ! yes, there is a still small voice
   Among the silent solitudes ;
To ears and hearts not deaf and cold
   It speaketh here distinct and clear :
He that hath eyes let him behold,
   He that hath ears, then let him hear.

TO MR JOHN TAYLOR.

Author of "Poems on Scottish subjects," a native of Ross-shire, and
now a settler in Michigan.

BARD of the North whose wiry form
   Was reared where towers the proud Ben Wyvis,
High where the waves of Cromarty
   Dance wild thro' cavern and crevice ;

Thou who when mists of mountains grand
   And scenes historic did surround thee,
Hast wrapt with fond and eager hand
   The Ossianic mantle round thee ;

Thy Harp and Lyre dost thou consign
    To deep and everlasting slumbers ?
And shall we listen but in vain
    To hear their sweetly swelling numbers ?

Dost thou forget the hills of Ross,
    The dark streams winding down the valleys ?
Dost thou refuse to sing of Bruce
    Or boast of glorious William Wallace ?

Hast thou no relish for the page
    Of bards who have bright laurels won
In by-gone or in present age—
    Burns, Cowper, Byron, Tennyson ?

Bard of the North ! and art thou dumb,
    When sunny days of Springtime come,
And when the heather is in bloom
    Around thy native highland home ?

Has the Autumnal eve and morn
    No high and holy thoughts for thee ?
And is the Wintry tempest shorn
    Of grandeur and sublimity ?

Bard of the North, let not thy Lyre
    In deep oblivion slumber longer,
But wake with true poetic fire—
    To accents nobler, bolder, stronger.

Not with the powerful thunder peal
    Of noble patriotism only,
But with the strains that soothe and heal
    The hearts that are both sad and lonely.

Thou hast a mission, doubt it not,
    Though by the rich and great unheeded ;
If faithful to thy Lyre, I wot
    But little is their friendship needed.

For stern and stalwart Highlandmen
    Thy name and fame shall fondly cherish,
And in the homes of many a glen
    Thy memory shall never perish.

And at the last they'll mourn thy loss
   As they ne'er mourned for one before thee,
While all the lakes and streams of Ross
   Shall join the lamentation o'er thee.

LAIRD KEYDEN'S LAST WISH.

Sixty or seventy years ago there was no name more familiar to the people of Linton than that of Mr Keyden, laird of Lynedale, and it was during the period in which he held possession of that small but beautiful estate that great improvements were made upon it. Mr Keyden had long entertained an idea that scarcely any spot was or could be so beautiful, and he often expressed a wish that at death he should, without pomp or ceremony, be decently interred in the green spot at the extremity of his own garden. This is situated on the banks of the Lyne, just before it enters a deep rocky glen; and forms one of the most picturesque scenes in the locality.

WHEN I my weary eyes have closed in death's unbroken
   sleep,
The promise which you give me now you faithfully will keep,
It is about my burial! You are not pledged nor bound
To lay me in the churchyard or in consecrated ground.
You will not mock my memory with pompous burial train,
With sad insignia of grief so hollow and so vain;
No! Let my dust be laid to rest in this delightful glen,
By neighbours and acquaintances, by homely honest men.
Down by the fence where terminates my pleasant garden
   ground,
And close beside the winding stream where is a sweet green
   mound.
There oft the Spring and Summer flowers, so delicate and
   rare,
I've marked with keen and eager eye—I wish to slumber
   there.
You will erect no monument to mar the peaceful scene,
To scare the glorious sunbeams when they've kiss my grave
   so green;
The brier bush and hawthorn near—I wish them still to
   stand,
Altho', alas! their flowers must be culled by another hand.

The same sweet buds and flowers shall come when Spring
    and Summer call;
The stream shall waft the same sweet hymn adown its rocky
    hall;
The same delightful sunbeams shall as gently come and go,
When peaceful is my slumber in the narrow bed below.
Lynedale, delightful spot! ah, thou my joy thro' life hast
    been;
Why should we part when death shall close this fleeting
    earthly scene?
A ceaseless source of pleasure thou unto this heart of mine;
Why should I not at last in peace upon thy breast recline?

We may state, that the wish of Laird Keyden was not complied with,
his ashes being interred in an obscure and ill-kept corner of Linton
Churchyard, where a plain marble slab in the wall bears the following
simple inscription:—"In memory of William Keyden, Writer to the
Signet, third son of the Rev. William Keyden, minister of Penpont,
Dumfriesshire, who was born the 15th September 1763, and died on the
5th January 1826."

THE DAYS OF THE CROFTERS.

'TWAS trim an' trig, Rob Farquhar's rig, as kailyaird e'er
    could be,
'Twas bounded by the rustic brig, the hedge, an' hawthorn
    tree;
The bonnie burn that swept alang, an' wimpled doon the glen,
Aye seemed to sing its sweetest sang near Robin's gable en'.

It wasna big, Rob Farquhar's rig—four acres, little mair—
Yet mony a bonnie Summer's day did crummie nibble there,
And Autumn saw his tatties braw, an' turnips fresh an' green,
Nae better in the Lothians nor in Teviotdale were seen.

'Twas trim an' trig, Rob Farquhar's rig—the next was Davie
    Gray's;
Synd auld Will Weir, the pensioner, who wore the sojer's
    claes;
Then Sandy Lamb, wha lo'ed his dram; next douce auld
    Widow Cairns,
Wha foucht a noble battle for her fatherless wee bairns.

She proudly scorned the pauper's dole, and toiled baith late
    an' air',
That winsome lads an' lasses might be clad an' get their lear',
An' to the warld sent honest sons, an' lasses trig an' braw,
Sic as mak' Scotland loved at hame an' honoured far awa.

In vain we seek the hedge that marked the crofters' acres
    now ;
O' garden or o' hamestead snug nae trace is left, I trow ;
In vain the wistfu' e'e noo turns to seek for ocht this day
To mind us o' douce Widow Cairns, or kindly Davie Gray ;

Or Sojer Will, wi' martial air, or funny Sandy Lamb,
Wha used to sing baith late an' air' aye when he got the
    dram,
Yet kindly to the neebors a', wha werena sweer to tell
That Saunders wi' his follies aye was warst just for himsel'.

'Tis fifty years since last we saw the reek o' Davie's lum,
Or heard auld Saunders lilt his sang, or Willie beat the drum,
An' yet it seems as yesterday that we were romping bairns,
An' rinnin' out an' in the byre to couthie Widow Cairns.

Alas! what strange emotions lie unspoken, unrevealed,
To see the crofters' acres form a'e nameless widespread field,
The fertile furrows now upturned by strangers—uncouth
    men—
Wha little for that history care o' whilk they little ken.

MUSINGS OF AN OBSCURE POET.

Do I believe my name shall live
    When other names are dead,
That it shall not be in the grave
    Of deepest darkness hid ?
Do I presume my musings may
    My memory prolong,
And that the world will care to keep
    Some record of my song ?

And when this mystic dream is past,
　This fleeting tale is told,
Do I expect to be at last
　In Fame's bright list enrolled ?
When in the lone churchyard I sleep
　In our dear native glen,
Shall I be in remembrance kept
　More than my fellow men ?

Oh, no! for shrouded in the mists
　Of dark oblivion now,
Lie thoughts of many a manlier breast,
　And many a nobler brow ;
And Fame's proud hand hath oft refused
　The laurel wreath to twine
For those whose fingers swept the lyre
　More skilfully than mine.

Why do I hail then the wild storms
　Of the dark Winter's day ?
Why sing the Spring's delightful charms
　In many a nameless lay ?
Why so much love the Summer's flowers,
　Its sunshine and its glee ?
And why are Autumn's peaceful hours
　So precious unto me ?

It is because strange feelings dwell
　Deep-seated in my breast,
Love of the grand and beautiful
　That seeks to be exprest ;
Keen sympathies, and strong desires,
　And hopes that cheer and bless ;
And warm emotions which no power
　Can stifle or suppress.

And when I keenly ponder o'er
　The mighty bards of old,
I prize their precious pages more
　Than miser does his gold.

Yea, often do I thrust aside
    Life's sorrows, griefs, and cares,
To drink at that pure fount, for, oh!
    No fellowship like theirs.

And yet the ditties I have waked
    In gladness and in gloom
May reach the peasant in the field,
    The weaver at his loom!
May help to soothe some saddened heart
    In sorrow's doleful day;
Or brighter make some humble hearth,
    Where worth and virtue stay.

If so, my mission is fulfilled,
    And mine is meet reward!
Although beyond my native hills
    My name is never heard.
And thou whose smile hath won my love
    Through all the chequered past,
A joy and solace still shall prove
    While life's brief day shall last.

LYNEDALE IN OCTOBER.

FAIR art thou, Lynedale, when greeted with the firstlings
    of the Spring,
And its warblers bid the echoes of the rocky valleys ring;
When the primroses profusely deck thy banks, dear native
    stream,
Where we sought them 'neath the sunshine of our youth's
    delightful dream;
Yet thou art not shorn of beauty though the flowers have
    faded all—
Though October winds sigh sadly, and the brown and sere
    leaves fall.
And let others deem thee fairest 'mid the Summer's joyous
    reign,
When thy drapery of foliage all untarnished doth remain,
While the flow'rets of thy bosom still have power to charm
    and please,
And bestow their balmy odours on the softly sighing breeze;

When the blackbird's mellow ditty blends at morning's
    joyous call
With the ceaseless soothing music of the favourite water-
    fall.
Yet to me thou art most queenly in the mellow Autumn day,
Robed in richly varied vesture—the insignia of decay.
As in pensive mood we ponder on this wood-crowned rocky
    height,
Scanning scenes that thro' my bosom send a thrill of strange
    delight,
Where a thousand tints and tinges on the raptured vision
    break,
Yet this is the thought that only in my bosom they awake,
Tho' the artist oft hath striven all thy beauty to portray,
And the lowly bard hath o'er thee lifted many a nameless
    lay,
Yet the artist's hand falls feeble, and the minstrel's lay is
    cold,
For the story of thy beauty still remaineth all untold.

IN MEMORY OF THE LATE GEORGE M'LEISH.

Suggested by his portrait, in the possession of Mr Waddell, Edinburgh.

AGREEABLE surprise indeed!
That now I 'm privileged to read
The manly features of that face,
Familiar since my early days;
The visage of a friend, whose store
Of quaint and legendary lore
Oft wak'd the voice of jocund mirth
Around the cheerful cottage hearth,
And proved, with readiness and ease,
His power to fascinate and please;
And proud was I to learn and know
That thou didst on the canvas glow;
That I again should meet the glance
Of that majestic countenance,
As oft I 've met it long ago,
When gazing on thy noble brow,
Amid the joy of years gone by;

And, thanks to those through whose kind care
That privilege we with pleasure share;
Though, in the time that now remains,
We never more shall list thy strains.
A prince and mighty man wert thou
Among the brethren of the bow,
For few there were who took the field
So deftly armed—so deeply skilled,
Who did with pride so fondly prize
Our ancient Scottish melodies.
Few could unlock true beauty's shrine
With touch so delicate as thine,
Few deck with thee in grand array
"Loch Foyers" or "Birks of Invermay;"
Few plead with plaintive power like thee—
"Oh, Nannie, wilt thou gang wi' me?"
Or mourn "Lord Gregory's" maiden's doom,
Or tell how "Bothwell Bank" did bloom;
And very few like thee, indeed,
Could make the merry dancers speed,
And mirth and gladness duly raise
With Highland reels and quaint strathspeys,
That oft evoked the liveliest mirth
Among the clansmen of the north,
In brighter days, of better years,
When fewer were the people's fears,
And jealousies of harshest tone
Were all undreamed of and unknown,
And peace and comfort spread their sails
Where discontent reigns and prevails.
May light soon from the darkness come
To many a lonely island home;
And may no foul dark deed of shame
E'er stain the noble Highland name!

But now, to others it remains
The task of waking those sweet strains,
And, to disclose their beauties now,
Another arm must yield the bow,
And other tongues must now re-frame
The legends linked unto thy name.

IN MEMORY OF THE LATE GEORGE M'LEISH.

No more among the mountains bleak
The storm will pelt upon thy cheek,
As oft it has in bygone time,
When thou wert in thy stalwart prime.
No more, 'neath cloudless Summer sky,
The shepherd shall thy form descry
Beside some lonely mountain stream
That glittered 'neath the bright sunbeam,
Where thou, with cheerful, lightsome heart,
Peacefully plied the angler's art.
That long, long life of fourscore years,
With all its joys, and hopes, and fears,
Is past; and with it, as there ought,
Come proper times of sober thought
Which bid us contemplate its close
As crowned with measure of repose;
And when the weary wanderings cease
We bid the pilgrim "Rest in peace."

There may be those who scorn to read
This tribute to thy memory paid,
And why? Because thou wert while here
A houseless, homeless wanderer!
To me, howe'er, it matters not—
Of such reproach I'll bear the blot,
And glad would be if nothing more
There could be left beside my door;
Glad, if my name be ne'er beset
With more opprobrious epithet.
Yet hearts there are, both leal and true,
And generous bosoms not a few
In cottage low and mansion fair,
Who in such feelings duly share;
And if thy memory hath the power
To brighten one brief evening hour,
Then friendship, says the humble strain
Now waked, hath not been waked in vain.

THE BONNIE HAWTHORN.

Verses suggested by the passing sight of a beautiful hawthorn tree on
the banks of the Ayr.

"How rich the hawthorn's blossom!"—*Burns.*

THOUGH mony flowerets bud an' blaw
By leafy bower an' birken shaw,
I trow there's nane among them a'
    To match the bonnie hawthorn.

Though myriad blossoms burst an' spring
By siller stream and crystal spring,
There's nocht to match the clustering
    That crowns the bonnie hawthorn.

Though weel I lo'e the yellow broom,
The whins when opening in bloom,
Yet whaur hae they the sweet perfume
    That hovers o'er the hawthorn?

The gaudy rose that rears its head,
The violet drooping in the shade,
Though high the praise to them that's paid,
    Still higher to the hawthorn.

Through Summer's langest, latest days,
'Mang a' the flowers that busk the braes
Or skirt the stream that onward strays,
    There's nane to match the hawthorn.

The bard, to Scotland now so dear,
Wha's fame is spread baith far and near,
He marked an' saw wi' vision clear
    The beauties o' the hawthorn.

An' though he sung in thrillin' strains
Her haz'lly shaws an' briery dens,
Her burnies toddlin' doon her glens,
    He didna pass the hawthorn.

Ay, while his Highland Mary's name
Is cherished in ilk Scottish hame,
While lowes the fire o' Burns' fame,
    We'll love the bonnie hawthorn.

Ye lowlier bards that wake the lyre
An' seek to share the sacred fire,
See that ye touch the trembling wire
    Owre Scotland's bonnie hawthorn.

Sing sweetly o' ilk glen an' shaw,
Ilk river, stream, and waterfa',
Sing o' her wild flowers ane an' a',
    But dinna pass the hawthorn.

And while her thistle still shall wave,
While heathbells mark the martyr's grave,
May truest loves their memories leave
    Beneath the bonnie hawthorn.

TO J. LAURIE, ESQ., J.P., LAURIETON, NEW SOUTH WALES.

After reading "Songs from the Mountains," by Henry Kendall,* presented by Mr Laurie to the writer.

DEAR friend and brother on a distant shore,
Now that thy many wanderings are o'er,
Now that thy throbbing bosom findeth rest
'Mong friends to thee the kindest and the best ;
Accept my thanks, record my meed of praise
To thee o'er thy own Kendall's noble lays.
"Songs from the mountains," beautiful indeed—
Like sparkling stream from wintry fetters freed—
Now speeding on its way, majestic, grand,
Like to the Garry of our own dear land ;
Then resting calmly, like the placid lake,
When Autumn's suns of her a mirror make ;
Then waking into sweet and soothing tune—
As thou hast heard the Ayr and "bonny Doon."

* The late Henry Kendall, the eminent Australian poet, was an intimate friend of Mr Joseph Laurie of Laurieton, who has many interesting reminiscences of him that are likely one day to come to the public. Kendall died 1st August 1882, at the age of 41; and in the *Sydney Town and County Journal* of 4th December 1886, there is an interesting account of the inauguration of a monument lately erected over his ashes in the Church of England burying-ground there. The ceremony of unveiling was performed by Lord Carrington, other eminent personages taking part, and the whole was witnessed by a large assemblage of spectators.

Build high the tower—immortalise his name—
Or build it not, that name will live the same;
He who in tones prophetic, noble, grand,
Hath told the greatness of thy rising land,
And waked the harp of richly varying wires
To sing the city of a thousand spires—
He shall wax great, as ages onward glide,
And men and homes with thee are multiplied;
And future bards who wake thy country's lyre,
Shall praise his name and kindle at his fire.

Name not his failings, these were things of earth;
Record his fame, perpetuate his worth—
Those glorious talents that to him were given,
And powers of song—for these were gifts from heaven.

THE AULD MILL BARN.

AIR—" When the kye come hame."

YE 'LL join wi' me, my cronies a', in this my hamely sang;
The nicht is glidin' fast awa', an' sune we 'll hae to gang.
My theme it is nae far to seek, my lilt 's nae ill to learn,
For aye the owre-word o't shall be—the Auld Mill Barn.
   The Auld Mill Barn, the Auld Mill Barn,
  For aye the owre-word o't shall be—the Auld Mill Barn.

Oh, brawly ye can bring to mind the happy hours we 've seen,
When lad an' lass frae hill an' glen were gathered there
    at e'en,
When future toils or comin' ills gied us but sma' concern,
As merrily the dance gaed doon the Auld Mill Barn.
   The Auld Mill Barn, &c.

December nichts are dreary when the wind is loud an' high,
December nichts are eerie when nae moon is in the sky;
But what cared we how rough the blast, how dark the nicht
    an' dern,
When rallied 'neath its lowly roof—the Auld Mill Barn.
   The Auld Mill Barn, &c.

Nae princely pile in a' the land, nae palace licht an' fair,
Wi' turrets glitterin' in the sun, may aince wi' it compare;
Nor lordlings grand, nor leddies chaste, wi' titles no' to earn,
Can ever match the groups that graced the Auld Mill Barn.
    The Auld Mill Barn, &c.

I dinna care for gowd or gear, or men o' high degree;
The humble cot an' lowly lot hae rowth o' joys for me,
An' seldom will the lowe o' love or friendship ever burn
As brightly as when kindled in the Auld Mill Barn.
    The Auld Mill Barn, &c.

We 've a' oor times o' sunshine, an' oor days o' darkness
    drear,
But ne'er let 's slip true friendship's grip sae lang 's we
    sojourn here,
An' in oor glee an' gladness, an' amid misfortune stern,
We 'll cherish aye the mem'ries o' the Auld Mill Barn.
    The Auld Mill Barn, &c.

Then join wi' me, my cronies a', in this my hamely sang.
The nicht is glidin' fast awa' an' sune we 'll hae to gang;
My theme it is nae far to seek, my lilt 's nae ill to learn,
For aye the owre-word o't shall be—the Auld Mill Barn.
    The Auld Mill Barn, &c.

IF WEE WILLIE DEE!

YE maunna wake wee Willie yet,
    He 's sleepin' gey an' soon',
Just keep the curtains spread abreed,
    An' let the blind bide doon.
The lee-lang nicht he 's turned and tossed,
    As sick as bairn could be—
Hoo precious this sweet blink o' rest—
    O, if wee Willie dee!

I 've seen him whiles as ill langsyne,
    I strive still to believe ;
I 'm aiblins wrang when I repine,
    An' sinfu' when I grieve.

Yet, if we 're doomed to part, how sad
    The life I then maun dree,
The only joy an' hope I had—
    O, if wee Willie dee !

Yestreen when I lay doon to rest
    At midnicht's eerie hour,
He laid his headie on my breast,
    An' close to me did coure.
" Ye winna leave me, mither dear,
    Ther 'll naething fash wi' me,
When I lie cuddlin' cosie here "—
    O, if my Willie dee !

O, deep 's the darkness hoverin' owre
    Life's weary path this day,
An' Hope's sweet flower, in this sad hour,
    Is witherin' fast away.
Yet, aiblins He wha reigns aboon,
    Baith strength and grace may gie
To bear 't, an' say "Thy will be done,"
    If my wee Willie dee.

SANGS ABOOT PRINCE CHARLIE.

THE peacefu' shades o' gloamin' gray
Hae closed the darksome wintry day;
Our humble cottage hame let 's hae
    Lit up baith bricht an' rarely.
Let a' thing else be thrust aside,
That honour due to them be paid,
An' let the gloamin' fleetly glide
    Wi' sangs about Prince Charlie.

For aince leave Robbie Burns alane,
An' Tannahill, wi' pleasin' strain,
An' ither bards wha in their train
    Hae followed e'en richt fairly.
For aince the tunefu' lilt we 'll learn
Frae Jamie Hogg, or Lady Nairne,
Wha a' the grace could weel discern
    An' valour o' Prince Charlie.

We 'll meet him on the Western isle,
Where first his foot pressed Scottish soil,
When friends and followers the while
    Were numbering but sparely.
Thro' dales an' glens wi' him we 'll steal
To whaur he met wi' *wise Lochiel*,
Wha argued wi' sic tact and skeel
    Wi' dauntless young Prince Charlie.

Let 's gather in Glenfinnan's vale,
Where first upon the northern gale,
Unfurled like gracefu' swelling sail,
    His banner floated fairly :
We 'll mark how loyal bosoms burn,
An' hear upon the breezes borne
The joyous shout of fealty sworn
    To gallant young Prince Charlie.

Or, let us view the gathering clans
Upon the field of Prestonpans,
When foes that didna fear him aince
    Are routed quick an' rarely ;
An' mighty men to rin are fleet
Wi' tidin's o' their ain defeat,
An' vow that nae mair, air' or late,
    They 'll meddle wi' Prince Charlie.

Let 's hear the welcome leal an' loud
That rang where pompous courtiers bow'd,
An' bade the halls o' Holyrood
    Re-echo long an' rarely ;
For now the fairest o' the land
Were fain to kiss the Prince's hand,
The bravest proud to take their stand
    'Neath banner o' Prince Charlie.

Nor scornfully let 's turn aside
When owre the Borders Charlie gaed,
Success an' failure, light an' shade,
    Were mingled here richt sairly,

For discord in the camp did reign;
An' back to Scotland's hills again,
Richt sairly dauntoned, cam', I ween,
　　The followers o' Prince Charlie.

Wi' tearfu' eye and bated breath
We 'll stand by lone Culloden's heath,
And o'er the dreadful scene of death
　　We 'll sorrow richt sincerely.
Ah! never 'mid the battle fray
Of valour was more grand display,
And yet the day is lost for aye
　　To clansmen an' Prince Charlie.

Ah me! for valiant hearts that lie
On lone Culloden field to die,
A bloody Cumberland is nigh,
　　To mercy stranger fairly.
The furious shout, the boastfu' word,
Wi' prancer's hoof and vengefu' sword,
Nae scene mair dreadfu' on record—
　　Oh, waes me for Prince Charlie!

We 'll see thee drifted o'er the wave,
Or laid in lonely mountain cave,
A faithfu' fair one, young and brave,
　　To tend thee late an' early.
A halo rests o'er every scene,
On lonely shore, or mountain green,
Where thou, brave wanderer, hast been—
　　Alas for young Prince Charlie!

Thrice fifty years are nearly fled
Since dire Culloden's day of dread,
When numbered 'mong the valiant dead
　　Were brave hearts equall'd rarely;
But mony a sun shall rise an' set
O'er scenes where rival armies met,
Ere Scotia's nymphs and swains forget
　　The sangs aboot Prince Charlie.

WHEN WILLY WAS THE BAIRN.

It is a sang of bygane years
  That I wad choose to sing,
A sunbeam frae the chequered past
  That back I'd fondly bring.
I dinna brood owre blasted hopes,
  Or mourn misfortunes stern;
Oh, no! I sing the happy hours
  When Willy was the bairn.

The morning scenes o' wedded life,
  When cares were licht an' few,
When gowden dreams did still retain
  Some tinge o' native hue;
When future toils an' dreaded ills
  Gied us but sma' concern,
Sae ta'en were we wi' a' his wiles
  When Willy was the bairn.

Encradled there, wi' a' his charms,
  Methinks I see him noo,
His ruby lips, his rounded arms,
  His een o' heaven's ain blue.
My Jean, a lichtsome lass, wi' a'
  A mither's wark to learn,
Tho' nocht could e'er come wrang ava
  When Willy was the bairn.

An' merrily she wrought an' sang
  Frae mornin' until e'en,
An' oh! nae ither voice e'er rang
  Sae sweet as that o' Jean;
An' lilts that at a mither's knee
  In childhood she did learn,
A precious treasure proved to be
  When Willy was the bairn.

How sweet was aye the partin' kiss
  At morn's dim drowsy dawn,
Afore my feet had trod the wold,
  Or crossed the dewy lawn!

My constant thocht frae morn till nicht,
   How I the maist micht earn,
To keep them snug, an' bien, an' richt,
   When Willy was the bairn.

That modest little crib has rocked
   Sax bonnie bairns sin' syne—
A merry band, a goodly flock,
   Are Jeanie's noo, an' mine.
They 've a' been spared, nae blank 's been made,
   To leave oor hearts forfairn,
Like sunbeams sweet oor path they 've lit,
   Sin' Willy was the bairn.

It ne'er was mine to stray in search
   O' wild an' maddening mirth,
I 'm heartiest in my humble hame,
   An' by my ain sweet hearth.
Let ithers seek their joys elsewhere—
   Wi' that I 've nae concern—
I 'll seek them there an' find them where
   Wee Willy was the bairn.

WHEN DAYS O' HAIRST DRAW NEAR.

Verses suggested by the remark of a friend, that she was always reminded of her greatest earthly loss when the days o' Hairst drew near.

It 's aye a welcome time to me,
   The bricht an' sunny Spring,
The Summer too, when fairest flowers
   Their sweetest fragrance bring.
An' weel I like the Winter chill,
   Though stormy, stern, an' drear,
But dowie thochts this bosom thrill,
   When days o' hairst draw near.

Langsyne I liked richt weel to see
   The richly ripenin' grain,
When wavin' fields did greet the e'e
   Owre a' the smilin' plain,

Or watch the moon that rose serene,
   Majestic, calm, and clear;
But sairly changed is a' the scene
   When days o' hairst draw near.

They come to mind me o' a form
   That dwined and dowed awa'
Afore the flowers had tint their bloom
   Or leaves began to fa'.
The pairtin' cost me mony a pang,
   An' mony a sigh an' tear,
An' aye sin' syne seems a'-thing wrang
   When days o' hairst draw near.

September's silence kent my grief,
   For aft at peaceful eve
My bleeding bosom socht relief
   Beside that lowly grave ;
While in the dell around me fell
   The leaflets, brown and sere,
That kissed the bed, but newly made
   When days o' hairst drew near.

Though mony a lang, lang Simmer's sun,
   An' mony a Winter's snaw,
Hae come an' gane sin' owre my path
   Death's shadow then did fa',
Yet aft I speir—Can nocht be found
   This saddened heart to cheer ?
But fresh aye bleeds the tender wound
   When days o' hairst draw near.

It 's weel the trials o' oor lot
   Are graciously concealed
By Ane wha kens what 's best disclosed,
   An' what 's best unrevealed ;
A Friend that will baith help an' heal,
   If Him we seek an' fear ;
An' 'twerna sac, my heart wad fail
   When days o' hairst draw near.

FAMILIAR EPISTLE TO JOHN VEITCH, ESQ., LL.D.,

**Professor of Logic and Rhetoric in the University of Glasgow,
Author of numerous Poetical Works.**

WHEN I approach thee, learned Professor,
I trust ye 'll deem me nae transgressor,
As I in peaceful hour of leisure
Seek to express the sense of pleasure
That oft has been, and still is mine,
When revelling 'mang those lays of thine,
The mair, forsooth, when we 're sae fain
To name, an' claim thee as oor ain;
We 've watch'd thy steady, bright career
Thro' mony a change o' mony a year,
An' as we saw thee calmly climb
To height o' honour maist sublime,
We 've felt arise within the breast
A pride that would not be suppress'd,
An' like a loyal Tweeddale's son
We greet thee with a leal " Well done;"
An' bid warm hearts in every home
Be proud o' oor wee Sheriffdom.
What 's wealth or land, what 's gowd or gear,
Weighed in the scales 'gainst genius clear?
What 's worldly pomp, rank e'er sae high,
Compared wi' what wealth cannot buy?
What lordly Veitch in Dawyck's tower
That lolled away the fruitless hour,
Be 't sprightly son, or stately sire,
E'er won sic honours for our shire?
Or did around the name entwine
Sic laurels fair as now are thine?
A chaplet neither won nor worn
'Mang scenes where sounds the huntsman's horn,
Nor on the bloody fields of war;
Associations purer far
Are those that are beloved by thee:
The glorious fields of poesy,
With all the pleasures that belong
To learning, minstrelsy and song.

I 've often felt, I feel it yet,
A cause of genuine regret,
That ane sae worthy admiration
Is far aboon our humble station!
Altho' I readily agree
It 's aiblins better far for thee.
Hadst thou been my ain stamp' an' style,
A plain and simple "Son of Toil,"
I wad hae ask'd thee, *learned one*,
To come and see our ancient toon,
An' tak' a tour, ye needna doot,
'Mang streams an' mountains roond aboot,
Presentin' ye, as ye may ken,
Wi' freedom o' my " *But-an-ben* " ;
I 'd shown ye a' my strange nick-nacks,
Auld books, queer documents and tracts,
Wi' mony a minstrel and his lays,
Sic as ye 've studied a' yere days;
An' prouder far I 'd been, I trow,
Thus to hae made a guest o' you,
Than ye had been the Czar, or Shah,
Frae Petersburg or Persia.

A treat 'twad been to spend wi' you
Ae nicht oot-owre the ingle lowe ;
I dinna lang to hear ye speak
In Latin, Hebrew, or in Greek ;
Wi' politics we wadna meddle,
Nay, we wad string anither fiddle.
I 'd bid ye broach your wondrous store
O' ancient Border ballad lore
Frae minstrels o' the misty past,
Doon to the latest and the last,
Frae verse abrupt and shapeless rhymes,
That stood for song in darker times,
Down to the grand majestic lays
And polished verse of modern days.

An' as the bards we took in tow,
We 'd set oor fancies in a lowe,
As freely we exchanged our views

On Leyden's lays and Riddell's muse;
And Scott himsel', wha's magic wand
Shed lustre owre the border land;
An' last, not least, the wily rogue
An' wondrous dreamer, Jamie Hogg,
Wha's name shall live while siller rills
Meander 'mang the Yarrow hills,
An' sunbeams light the sylvan scene
'Mang Ettrick's lonely mountains green,
Where oft his stalwart form was laid
To slumber in his Auld Grey Plaid.
An' oh ! sic dreams are seldom heard
As they're tauld by "The Mountain Bard."

Nor wad we aince ignore the claim
O' mony a lesser noted name,
Of lowlier vot'ries of the lyre,
Who sought to kindle at their fire.

I doot na but we twa wad haen
A hasty trip across the main,
To spend an' hour wi' meikle zest
Amang the poets o' the West;
Those noble bards that struck the key
Of Freedom and of Liberty,
Who sought deep darkness to dispel,
And ring foul slavery's funeral knell:
Bryant and Whittier ! true as steel;
And Longfellow, the pure and leal;
And "Fitzgreen Halleck !" he who shared
Sic generous love for Scotia's bard,
An' left the piled leaves of the West
To linger where his ashes rest.
A memorable Autumn noon
Was that he spent by bonnie Doon,
And in his honour waked a strain
But little short o' "*Burns's ain.*"

Yet wherefore thus prolong my scribble
To length that may but prove a trouble?

Let me express but what I feel,
My warmest wishes for your weal.
Be 't distant far that dolefu' day
When ye nae mair shall seek to stray
Owre Cademuir hill, to scan wi' care
The varied landscape rich an' rare ;
Blackhouse' blue heights sae far awa',
The Meldon's peaks or Dollar Law,
And mony a hill whose name is heard
Familiar as a household word ;
When tongue and pen shall cease to tell
O' Flowers that bloom in Newby dell,
Or paint the legendary tale
Of Merlin's grave and lone Powsail ;
Or burnish bright their blood-stain'd swords
Drummebyier's furious feudal lords,
By transcript of those days of dool
When wealth gave power to fiend or fool,
And might, not right, did reign and rule ;
When dearest scenes and fairest form
For thee possess no power to charm ;
When joyless seems Tweed's crystal tide,
And lyre and pen are laid aside,
And thou shalt cease and that for ever,
Thy songs of our dear classic river,—
E'en as right many a lesser stream,
That glitters 'neath Sol's glorious beam,
To Tweed anon doth tribute pay,
From lonely glen and hillside grey,
As she pursues her onward way;
So let her bard due praise receive
From lowlier ones their lays that weave
Among the mountains bold and grand
That beautify our border land.
For this my warblings I renew
To pay to thee the tribute due,
And proudly take my place 'mang them
Who prize thy gifts, and love thy name.

IT WAS HERE.

It was here, my loved, my fairest—it was here that first
    we met,
When the reaper's merry song had ceased and the Autumn
    sun had set
'Mid the weird unbroken silence reigning these wild glens
    among,
Where the streamlet from the mountain wakes its lowest,
    softest song.

It was here, fair love, we lingered with a pleasant, fond delay,
Till the queen of night had risen o'er yon mountains far
    away,
Lighting up the glassy lakelet and the streamlet in the wood,
And the lonely pathway winding thro' the blissful solitude.

It was here, fair love, we parted, here that soft white hand of
    thine
After many a pledge and promise was so fondly clasped in
    mine;
Here amid the unsung beauty of this wild romantic dell
First I felt the pain of parting, first I heard thee say,
    Farewell.

Autumn's latest flowers are faded, Autumn's latest songs
    are sung,
Wintry winds are wildly wailing lone and leafless woods
    among.
What of all the hallowed memories of this wild romantic
    dell,
And that moonlight Autumn evening! 'tis not mine alone
    to tell.

It was here a flame was kindled in this leal and faithful
    heart,
O'er which Time, that dire destroyer, hath no power to act
    his part.
As unquenched that love remaineth, so unchanged that love
    will be:
Say, my fairest one and dearest, can that tale be told by thee?

H

EPISTLE TO A. R., A BROTHER POET.

A WELCOME waits the simple voice
  From Lyne's fair vale that cometh,
This fragment of such melodies
  As oft thy brother frameth;

As in the Summer's joyous prime,
  With sight and sound elated,
I seek once more to have my rhyme
  To Friendship dedicated;

A thousand fair and beauteous flowers
  Now by my pathway springing—
A thousand birds within the bowers
  Their ditties sweetly singing—

Awake the memories of that hour
  When first, dear friend, I met thee,
And with a pleasant secret power
  Forbid that I forget thee;

And weeks, and months, and years have sped,
  And still the spell remaineth,
Unchanged, save that the opening flower
  A brighter bloom attaineth;

Thus, in the future, may the stream
  Become a noble river,
To us more than a pleasing dream,
  Be it "a joy for ever."

And as we seek the peaceful glens,
  In pensive mood to wander,
Where richest foliage drapes the scenes,
  And clearest streams meander.

Among the Poets of the past
  We'll revel free and often;
And fellowship of kindred hearts
  The cares of life will soften.

Well, may it be with thine and thee,
   May Heaven's bright smile be o'er thee,
'Mid all the duties, griefs, and joys,
   Dear friend, that are before thee;

And while thy winsome olive plants
   Thy inmost bosom gladden,
With all their cares, and needs, and wants,
   May no dark cloud thee sadden.

But, 'mid the sunshine of those souls
   That proudly rally round thee,
May I in future find thee still
   As happy as I 've found thee !

Rich—not in gold nor fertile fields,
   That worldlings' hearts seek rest in ;
But in such treasure-trove as yields
   A joy both pure and lasting.

CLERICAL WITS.

THE LATE REV. HAMILTON PAUL.*

TWENTY-EIGHT years have come and gone since that day when there was such an anxiety among the villagers of Broughton, and an unusually large and most respectable train of funeral attendants followed to their last resting-place the mortal remains of one whose form and figure had been familiar in the district for nearly half a century. We refer to the Rev. Hamilton Paul, minister of the united parishes of Broughton, Kilbucho, and Glenholm, a gentleman in whom there met and mingled so many and so varied qualities, singling him out in a very conspicuous manner from the generality of those occupying a similar position with himself, and by which his name and memory are and will be fondly cherished in the glens and the homes of Tweeddale.

The subject of this brief notice was born at Dailly, in Ayrshire, in 1773, and, as can be said of many an illustrious Scotchman, he received the rudiments of his education at the Parish School. His academical studies were finished at the University of Glasgow, where he was the college friend and intimate companion of Thomas Campbell, author of "The Pleasures of Hope," and with whom he kept up a correspondence for a long period. Of his history from this time till his settlement in Broughton little is known. He was for some time editor, as also proprietor, of a provincial newspaper, and to this period belongs the first of those hits, for which, in after life, he was so famous. On leaving Ayr, he advertised a sermon to the young ladies of the town, when, to the astonishment of his audience, he chose as his text the words from Acts xx. and 37, "And they all wept sore, and fell upon Paul's neck and kissed him."

We may here, however, note a fact that is not so generally known, viz., that Mr Paul had been promised the living of

* From a paper given at one of the weekly meetings of the West Linton Mutual Improvement Association, six years ago.

an important parish in Ayrshire, and that the parishioners looked forward, and that with a feeling of interest, to his future settlement among them. This is substantiated by letters on the subject which have fallen into the possession of the writer, though evidently an earlier vacancy was the means of overturning the arrangement referred to.

Mr Paul's predecessor in the ministry of the united parishes was Mr Porteous, who forms one of the subjects of comment in Simpson's "Memoirs of Eccentric Worth." Mr Porteous was a man of very strict abstemious habits, and it is said that Mr Paul, on his appointment to the benefice in 1813, said he meant to imitate his predecessor in one thing only, and that was his celibacy. This he did, for he remained unmarried all his life, which circumstance formed the subject of a song by Mr Paul, dealing with the names of the various members of the Presbytery of Biggar, of which he was a member, and entitled, "A'body's like to get married but me."

The above song was long popular in the surrounding parishes, and is occasionally heard from some of the more elderly persons who can recall the faces of those with whose history it deals.

On the occasion of the ordination of the Rev. Mr Meek to the parish of Dunsyre, he, acting as officiating clergyman, chose as his text Matthew v. 5—"Blessed are the *meek*;" and when he introduced Mr Hope to the parish of Lamington, he chose for his text the words,—"The *hope* set before them."

On one occasion he was preaching for Dr Aiton at Dolphinton. In the absence of the said clergyman, the manse was shut up, and Mr Paul, after travelling a good long journey, ascended the pulpit without even having partaken of a drink of water. His text was—"I say unto you, nay; but except ye repent ye shall all likewise perish," which words were repeated at frequent intervals in the discourse. After having spoken for some time, he became faintish and pale, and one of the elders perceiving this went up to the side of the pulpit, and advised him to sit down for a little. Mr Paul, without distorting his remarks, looked over the pulpit and repeated emphatically—"I say unto you, *nay*; but except *ye* repent ye shall all likewise perish." After a few sentences, however, he stated to the congregation that he did feel a little unwell. He had come a long journey that morning and found the manse locked up, and asked the congregation to favour him by singing a psalm, when, he said, he had no doubt he would be able to proceed with his discourse, which he afterwards did with his usual readiness.

A friend, calling on him, told him he was kindly enquired for by a friend in Sanquhar, a Mr Weir. "Ay, ay," replied Mr Paul, "an' weel may he wear."

At a friendly meeting in Broughton Manse he had present Mr Taylor, minister of Drummelzier; Mr Gardiner, son of the minister of Tweedsmuir; Mr Smith, also a cleric; Miss Loch of Rachan; and two gentlemen of the name of Millar. Taking advantage of the group, Mr Paul said he never had a more useful company in his house at one time—a Taylor, a Smith, a Gardiner, and no less than two Millars. "I guess," said one of the company, "you may have difficulty in finding water for two Millars."—"How can I have that," replied Mr Paul, exultantly pointing to Miss Loch of Rachan, "when I have a Loch at my right hand ? "

On one occasion, when dining in the mansion-house of one of the heritors of the parish, a foppish young gentleman seated next to him wished to make very free with him, and addressed the then old man—"Mr Paul, you have very long nails just now."—"I daresay I have," he replied in an indifferent manner. The same words were repeated, and received a similar reply. "I wonder very much to see you wearing them so long."—"Ye needna wonder at that," Mr Paul replied; "I'm just become a kind o' Nebuchadnezzar, eating wi' the beasts o' the field."

The Scottish manse has not unfrequently been the nursery of artistic skill and genius, as well as the source of intellectual and literary greatness.

Howe, the celebrated painter, was a son of the Rev. W. Howe, minister of Skirling, and like Sir David Wilkie, who was reared in the manse of Cults, the scenes among which he was reared were the first to call forth the early proofs of genius. For as "A Scene at Pitlessie Fair" was one of his first performances which attracted attention, so with Howe, one of whose earliest productions, according to Dr Hunter, was "A Skirling Fair and Stallion Show."

On one occasion, when Howe was a visitor at Broughton Manse, the customary courtesies past, Mr Paul said to him, "An' what are ye after the day—Drawin', I'se warrant?"—"Oh, yes," replied Howe, "drawin' to be sure."—"An' what hae ye been committin' to paper to-day?"—"I've been drawin' a horse, sir."—"Drawin' a horse! Wad it no' been better if he had been drawin' a cart on sic a fine harvest day, when every ane's busier than his neebor?"—"Maybe it wad," replied Howe, "but in that case I might be comin' on ye for corn."—"I've nae doot," replied Mr Paul, "ye might be comin' on me for that, an' mair than that. I've aye the notion you chaps are waur to slocken than to fill."

When visiting some friends in Linton, Mr Paul called, among others, on an old woman, who had prepared herself for his visit, and who asked him, "Mr Paul, will ye tak' a glass o' spirits?"—"Oh, atweel, gudewife, I may tak' it, but it's only flinging water on a droon't moose."

At a meeting of the Presbytery of Biggar, of which he was a member, he entered the same considerably behind time and saluted them with the words, "Here comes the *late* Mr Paul of Broughton."

On arriving at Mossfennan House on one occasion with Miss Welsh, who had been on a visit at the manse, Mr Welsh observed some particles of wool on his coat, and said, "Mr Paul, ye're a' 'oo'."—"How can I be otherwise?" he replied, "Miss Welsh has woo'd me a' the road up."

In the parishes of which he was minister, there were several eccentric characters, with whose peculiarities he was greatly amused. Returning one evening from a parochial visitation, he called on one of these, and found him sitting on the front of his bed playing the fiddle. "Ye're taking a tune, William?" said Mr Paul. "Oh, ay, sir," was the reply. "I think I heard ye playing when I passed the back of the house this morning?"—"Oh, very likely, sir."—"Have ye just been playing a' day, then?" asked the minister. "Ay, just that," was the reply. "Ye maun play a great deal, surely, William?"—"Oh, 'deed div I, sir; in fact I've little else to do, sir."—"And, d'ye never get off the tune, William?"—"Ay, mony a time." "Then how do ye act in these circumstances?" "Oh, *I juist ca' awa' till I come on't again,* sir."

Mr Paul was a welcome guest at those merrymakings which were of so frequent occurrence in country parishes in past years, and took an active part in the national game of curling and other innocent rural amusements.   Poetry was always a favourite recreation and study of his; and from time to time his effusions appeared in the leading journals of the day.   A fair specimen of his powers may be read in Professor Wilson's edition of Burns's Works in an ode to the memory of Burns, of whom he was a most ardent admirer.   It is also worthy of notice that, among the other works he wrote, was a Biography of Robert Burns.

A small collection of poems, entitled "A Foretaste of Pleasant Things," was published by him and dedicated to his brethren of the Presbytery of Biggar.   But, besides this, as has been said, his general productions had appeared in newspapers and magazines for a period of more than half a century.

We must not here omit to mention that the Statistical Account of the united parishes of which he was minister, has been always regarded by judges as amongst the best, and most elaborate, of any of the contributions to that work published in 1834.

The manse of Broughton was the resort of many of the learned and eminent men of the day, amongst whom we may mention Lord Cockburn, as also Professor Wilson, who was a regular visitor, and who found in the minister of Broughton a most interesting companion.   Of his manse it could safely be said—

"His house was known to all the vagrant train;"

for in him the poor found an unchanging friend, and the case was a very doubtful one, indeed, where his sympathy and support could not be commanded.   This was a fact pretty well known and frequently taken advantage of.

When it was known that he was to occupy the pulpit of any of the neighbouring parishes, there was generally a good sprinkling of strangers to see and hear the clergyman of whom so many curious anecdotes were told.   Such a visit on the part of the curious, however, generally ended in disappointment, for there was nothing observably odd in his pulpit appearances.   In fact the opposite was the case, particularly in the latter years of his life, when his appearance in the pulpit was very interesting : a high, intelligent brow, shaggy eye-brows, and locks white as silver resting upon his shoulders ; a calm, composed, and rather melancholy air, and, what tickled the strangers through the course of his carefully prepared sermon, a slight break down at frequent intervals, when, after a hasty wipe of his eyes with his hand, his discourse was proceeded with, readily and fluently.

In the later years of his life, he had to avail himself of the services of one assistant after another ; among whom he had for some time a very popular preacher, the Rev. Mr Riach, afterwards minister of Pencaitland, and now of the "Robertson Memorial Church," in Edinburgh. It was during the period of his assistantship, when the popularity of the young preacher brought many worshippers from the surrounding parishes, that Mr Paul was taunted with the large attendance. "Are you aware the gigs are flyin' in a' directions every Sunday mornin'?" said a friend to him, in a joke. "Oh, yes," replied Mr Paul, "perfectly well aware. A new broom sweeps clean, but if I could get filling the pulpit mysel' five or six Sundays a' rinnin', I will be bound ye I wad preach them a' back to their ain parishes."

The last of the circle of clergymen with whom he was in closest intimacy, were the Rev. Dr Christison of Biggar, and the Rev. Mr Proudfoot of Culter ; and all that remains to remind us of Mr Paul is the decent monumental stone, with simple inscription, which marks the spot where his ashes repose, close by the ruins of the old Parish Church, in the quiet and unpretending churchyard of Broughton. His death took place on the 28th February 1854. For several years previous, Mr Paul withdrew in a great measure from society, making a public appearance only occasionally when filling the pulpit of a neighbouring Parish Church, but retaining all his mental faculties to the last.

The foregoing anecdotes are a mere selection from those still told of him, and we have confined ourselves almost exclusively to those heard from his own lips, keeping aloof, as far as in our power, from those given by Dr Hunter in "Biggar and the House of Fleming."

We have in the course of these remarks referred to his

poetical works in general, but such a notice would be very imperfect without at least a reference to his local poems. These were composed from time to time during nearly the whole of his residence in the county, and were written on every conceivable subject; in fact, there was scarcely an event of any interest which occurred in his own, or in the surrounding parishes, which did not tempt his humble muse to take flight. Many of these pieces were preserved by the inhabitants without the aid of printing, owing doubtless to their being very closely connected with incidents and events which of themselves were memorable and interesting.

The following piece, composed by him when returning from the funeral, at Tweedsmuir, of Caroline Welsh, a young woman of great amiability, and possessed of great personal attractions, was recited to me by a person 80 years of age, who, knowing the young lady, had preserved them in her memory, though the death took place 50 years ago :—

> Sleep on, sweet maid ; thy father's silent woe,
> Thy brother's sorrow, and thy sister's tears,
> Which unremittingly for thee do flow—
> Torn from them in thy early blooming years—
> Can ne'er awake thee to the realms of light.
> Thy gentle spirit now hath winged its way,
> Thine eye, so radiant with its beauty bright,
> Is sunk in darkness and consigned to clay.
>
> Where Tweed and Talla mix their kindred stream,
> The green turf presses on thy blameless breast,
> No midnight phantom, no intrusive dream,
> Disturb thy shade, or thy repose molest.
> Sleep on, sweep maid, while evening dews descend
> On flowerets sweet around thy grassy grave,
> Our steps toward that hallowed spot we'll wend,
> And mix our tears with Tweed's sad running wave.

It is not necessary to make quotations from any of his well-known pieces, such as "A'body's like to get married but me;" or, as he calls it, "The Presbytery Garland;" but as we have given one short piece, pointing back to an early period of his ministry, we may now give one written near its close. It is an apology sent when invited to a dinner in connection with the christening of a son of Sir G. Graham Montgomery, Bart., and addressed to Mr Wm. Aitchison, chairman, and is interesting because it brings so much individuality to the surface, and also that it was the last, or among the last, of his pieces which appeared in the local papers, he being then seventy-seven years of age.

Poortith-an' eild, a matchless pair,
Have made me wear a coat threadbare,
And tried, with many a fiend-like snare,
    To sink me in the earth.
Yet, spite of their united powers,
I still delight 'mong greenwood bow'rs
To strew my path with fragrant flow'rs,
    And welcome harmless mirth.

Now, Willie, as the glass goes round
Let three times three of cheers resound,
Till echo bid the roof rebound
    To the uproarious joy;
And as ye burn with friendship's flame,
Blend the Montgomery with the Graham,
While the Right Reverend tells the name
    Of the dear infant boy.

When first Tweed's waters met my view,
To his great-grandsire's hall I flew,
And saw the Chief his life renew
    Amid a blooming throng
Of youths, adorn'd with graces rare,
And maidens lovely, debonair;
Who, crowding round his elbow-chair,
    His hours of bliss prolong.

His grandsire was a friend to me,
His sire I 've dandled on my knee;
And tho' I shall not live to see
    Himself to manhood spring—
Tho' I can neither sing nor dance,
And hear the chariot wheels advance,
I 'll do my best within the manse
    To gar the rafters ring.

Since my life's frolic era 's o'er,
I must not try as heretofore
To set the table in a roar,
     But seek a place of rest;
A chamber, just six feet by three,
Will prove a bed of down to me,
Whence I may rise by Heaven's decree
     To mingle with the blest.

BROUGHTON MANSE, 1st April, 1850.

THE REV. DR AITON.

THE compact, quiet, and well-cultivated little parish of Dolphinton, on the eastern extremity of Lanarkshire, has frequently secured for the discharge of its pastorate men superior to those who filled the pulpits in parishes of greater importance. Some of them have been prominent as ecclesiastics, others eminent and exemplary as philanthropists, while a third party have been notable for their contributions to the literature of our country.

The Rev. James Bowie, whose name stands out prominently on account of his liberal bequest to the parishioners, was succeeded by the Rev. Mr M'Courtney ; the next was the Rev. Mr Fergusson, who was succeeded by the Rev. Dr. Gordon, after whose sudden death in 1813 the charge was presented to the Rev. Mr Russell, minister of Dunsyre, who died after an incumbency of ten years in the parish of Dolphinton. Then the patron bestowed the living upon a young man whose literary tastes had attracted him and awakened his admiration, namely, the Rev. John Aiton, the subject of our remarks, who was ordained minister of Dolphinton in 1824.

It is not, however, our intention to rehearse or dwell upon the numerous works of which he was author, neither do we intend to reproduce the reminiscences of the Disruption period, but we mean to collect and husband a few of those anecdotes which were associated with his name in his ordinary parochial labours, more especially towards the close of his protracted ministry in the quiet parish of Dolphinton.

The early years of the Doctor's ministry were not characterised by any very marked publicity of his name, further than his well-known devotion to literary pursuits; but occasionally he came before the public on account of some notable sermon on the prophecies, preached in some of the neighbouring parish churches, or some very quaint anecdote or witty reply. He was frequently asked to officiate, both in large towns and in rural parishes, in the way of preaching funeral sermons, for which he was believed to have a great aptitude. On one occasion after the funeral sermon over the minister of a country parish, he had not got divested of gown and bands when the eldest daughter of the deceased clergyman accosted him with the greeting—"Oh, Doctor, I'm very much disappointed with you to-day."—"I am very sorry to hear that, but on what ground rests your disappointment?"—"Well," she replied, "I expected you would have something far more flattering to have said about father."—"I always make it my aim to keep as near the truth as is possible," rejoined the Doctor. A few days afterwards he met a farmer who had been present—"D'ye mean to say that the one-half ye said aboot the minister on Sunday last was true?"—"Now," replied the Doctor, "I have had insinuations from both sides; I think, after all, I must have been very near the bit."

On one occasion he had been assisting at the table service of a parish in Lanarkshire and was about to leave, when he came outside the manse and called to his man-servant—"Dinna yoke the beast, Tam; dinna yoke yet."—"What's wrang?" asked his servant, "what's wrang?"—"Plenty wrang," said the doctor; "there's a body has come to preach the evening sermon—ane o' the kind that disna cairry his sermon in his head but in his pouch—unfortunately on this occasion he has neither got it in the ane or the ither, and I'll hae tae tak' the poopit mysel'. I wadna gi'e a fardin' for a man that couldna stand up and preach a sermon at half-an-hour's warnin'!"

One Sunday evening, after delivering a lecture in Biggar Kirk on the evils of Popery, the Rev. Mr Christison said—"Doctor, I never was more thankful to hear your lecture brought to a close."—"And for what reason?"—"Because," replied Christison, "there were a good number present who had little sympathy with your remarks on purgatory."—"Oh, indeed," replied the Doctor, "I only wish I had known, I wad hae gi'en them a little mair o' the 'blue lowes.'"

At a social meeting of a few of the clergy the Rev. Mr Wilson of Walston told a story that excited the wonder of the company, when the Doctor jeeringly said—"Ah, Wilson, Wilson, it's very easy seeing ye've been at the forge!" Rev. Mr Wilson was a blacksmith in early life.

The Doctor was one day officiating in the Parish Church of Newland, for the Rev. Mr Charteris, and had an intimation left to him to read. It was to the following effect:— "The Rev. Mr Charteris will visit on Tuesday at Easter and Wester Deanshouses and Roodenlees, and on Thursday at Whim, Cowdenburn, and Kelty Green." The Doctor said—"I am requested to intimate your pastor will visit on Tuesday at Easter and Wester Deanshouses and Roodenlees, and on Thursday at Whim, Cowdenburn, and some other place which I cannot with certainty make out. I can see, however," said the Doctor, "it is something green."

On one occasion he had engaged in a lively discussion on Church and State with a parishioner who was an ardent Dissenter. Next day he called on him to ask if he would come to the manse and assist with the in-putting of his hay stack. "With the greatest pleasure," said the man. "Very good," said the Doctor, "very good. Far better to build up the minister's hay stack than to pull down the venerable Kirk."

Thirty years ago, when coaching was the only means of conveyance from Edinburgh to West Linton, the Doctor one Saturday night went forward to claim a seat at the time of the departure of the coach from the Register. He was told, however, that it was full. The Doctor got excited and began to speak rather loudly, when a farmer reproving him, said—"Keep cool, Doctor, keep cool; remember it's Hallow Fair."— "Hallow here or Hallow there," he replied, "it's to be a very unhallowed affair if I lose my seat and have to undertake a pilgrimage of twenty miles on foot."

After having preached one Sabbath in the Parish Church of Kirkurd, he was met one day by a Dissenting friend, who addressed him in terms like the following:—"Weel, Doctor! I gaed ance errand to Kirkurd to hear ye on

Sunday."—"Oh, indeed!" said the Doctor; "I hope ye was edified?"—"Weel, I cannot say I was."—"I am sorry for that," said the Doctor. "What was defective in my discourse?"—"Weel, I can only say I thought ye made very little o' Jephtha's daughter."—"Quite sound!" replied the doctor; "quite sound! What did I ken about Jephtha's daughter ony mair than Jephtha's daughter kent about me?"

During the long period of his incumbency in Dolphinton, the office of beadle rested on the shoulders of Jamie Walker, the tailor, with whom the Doctor used the greatest familiarity, both out of the church and inside as well, as the following anecdote will show;—The Doctor was one day proceeding with his sermon when, through a broken pane in one of the skylights over the pulpit, the wind blew the small piece of paper on which he had his headings pencilled down, into the square seat on the left of the pulpit, where Jamie Walker's face and form were so familiar. The doctor looked over the pulpit and said, "James, will ye kindly hand me up my notes? No response, however, was made. Again the Doctor looked over the pulpit, and spoke a little louder, as he observed James was just awakening from a comfortable snooze. "James Walker, will ye hand me up my notes? I feel I cannot get on comfortably in their absence." "Oh, I'll hand ye them up, sir," said James, "but d'ye no think it's high time ye was bringing the thing to a bearing?"

One Saturday the minister called on James, who was at the time busily engaged in making a pair of trousers. James lifted up his head and asked—"What are ye gaun to be on the morn, Doctor? The flood, I'se warrant," (the Doctor was at that time lecturing through the book of Genesis.) "Very likely, James; very likely. When a body begins a job they maun finish't if they expect to have credit by it; ye'll ken by yersel, James."—"True," rejoined James; "but ye've splashed a lang time i' the water noo."—"Oh ay, James, lad; but I'll come out it some day in a hurry and flap my wings wi' a feelin' o' pride. Guid day, James; guid day."

On one occasion a hive of bees belonging to him took up their position in the belfry of the Episcopal Chapel, and when informed of it the Doctor said—"If it had been that of Mountain-cross Meeting-House, or of Knocknowes Free Kirk, I could have understood it; but the belfry of the Episcopal Chapel seems to me ominous indeed." When one day informed that the Cleggs had left and joined the Free Church, he jocularly replied—"Oh, there's nae fear o' them. The Cleggs will come back in their season." The family referred to was that of Cleghorn, and in his prognostications the Doctor was perfectly right, for they were found in his congregation at the close of his ministry.

A heritor in the neighbouring parish met him one day, and asked if he had seen the Episcopal Chapel in course of erection, and what he thought of it. "Yes," said the Doctor, "I have seen it, and there is one mistake you have made I think.'—"Indeed," said the gentleman, "and what is it?" "You ought to have built it nearer the burn, for if it fails in its object, as it is likely it will, you could have turned it into a meal mill. You have an outshoot which would do first-rate for the water wheel."

A friend of his own, an old teacher from Linton, used occasionally to visit Dr Aiton, and once he was enjoying a walk through the churchyard along with the Doctor and his second wife, when the Doctor showed his friend where he wished to lie, on the left side of his first wife. "And where am I to be laid?" asked Mrs Aiton. "On my left side again," said the Doctor, and with a waggish smile whispered in the ear of his friend—"Then I'll be atween the deil and the deep sea."

The manse of Dolphinton is at a considerable distance from the little church, and it was the system in Dr Aiton's time, as it is still, to ring the bell when the minister leaves the manse, and, after an interval, to ring it again when he is ascending the brae to the churchyard, this being termed "the ringin'-in bell." The friend from Linton to whom we have already referred visited him in his last illness, and on being ushered into his room eagerly inquired of him—"What's this, Doctor, what's this that has overtaken ye noo?"—"Ah, Mr Paterson," replied the Doctor, "this is just the ringin'-in bell."

Mr Gray of Kirkurd, who had compiled a pamphlet entitled the "Life of Joseph," and who had entrusted the sale of the book to Mr Noble, of Knocknowes, who, owing to the dull sale, had reduced the price from 9d to 6d, had occasionally hard hits at Dr Aiton of Dolphinton. The Doctor, however, waited his chance to retaliate, and he won in this way :—Being invited by Mr Gray to a school examination in this reverend gentleman's parish, the Doctor proceeded on foot on the day set forth, and on his way to the school overtook several boys. Dr Aiton being a free jovial gentleman soon got into conversation, and his first question was, " Where are you going?" One of the boys replied that they were going to the Parish School. " It's oor examination." The Doctor at once made himself known as being a minister, and told them that he intended being at the examination along with several other ministers. Further on the road he asked the boy who had been spokesman if he could tell him who sold Joseph. The boy smartly replied, " His brethren."—" Now," says the Doctor, " here is half-a-crown for you, my good boy. I will put that question to you to-day at the examination. I will ask you, " Who sold Joseph?" You will say, " Wm. Noble, Knocknowes." I will then ask you, " For how much did he sell him?"—You will reply, " He set him up at 9d, but he is reduced to 6d now." The questions were put and answered, and Mr Gray was in such a rage that he left the examination of the school, crying out as he left—" Who wrote the lies about the Holy Land? Let the Doctor answer that!"

The anecdotes generally told regarding the person whose name we have used are so frequently of a humorous character that people are apt to believe that it was only on account of his humour that his name has come so prominently into notice. But the same composition which occasionally embraced a little of the humorous and eccentric was more frequently distinguished for happy hits, and for passages of great beauty, as the following will in some measure prove :— The Doctor was assisting at a Communion in West Linton. When delivering his sermon, in the evening, a violent thunderstorm broke over the locality, and he had frequently to pause till the peal was over. It was evident that the worshippers expected the Doctor would, in his readiness, refer to the solemnity of the occasion. This, however, he did not do in the course of his sermon ; but, after giving

out a few verses of the 97th Psalm—which includes the
following :—

> Fire goes before Him, and His foes
> It burns up round about ;
> His lightnings lighten did the world,
> Earth saw and shook throughout—

he proceeded with the closing prayer as follows :—"Oh
thou great and mysterious Being, with whom one day is as
a thousand years, and to whom a thousand years are as one
day; do Thou enable us, the creatures of a day who
are crushed before the moth, to realise alike our own
insignificance, and Thy glorious and Thy infinite majesty.
And since Thou hast at this time brought us face to face
with Thy dread omnipotence, enable us with one accord
to ascribe to Thee the glory due unto Thy name; 'Give
unto the Lord, oh ye mighty ; give unto the Lord glory
and strength.'"   After repeating, with great composure, and
solemnity, the whole of the 29th Psalm, he closed his
devotional reference by praying that all present might
take shelter under the wings of Him who at first
stretched out the heavens as a curtain, and who laid the
foundations of the earth, when the morning stars sang
together, and all the sons of God shouted for joy, so that
they might find their safety in Him hereafter, when the
heavens and the earth should pass away.
     Although his method of preaching was conversational
and homely, exaggerations on this point have frequently
been circulated and believed ; and perhaps most prominently
in connection with an illness from which he suffered several
years before his death, caused through the sting of a mos-
quito or other venomous fly. Despairing of his recovery,
he did undoubtedly preach a farewell sermon to his parishioners in a sitting posture.   Being present on the occasion,
however, we can testify there was nothing in that service
to excite merriment, or call forth hostile criticism, but the
opposite.   The discourse was a running commentary on
the 17th chapter of Job, beginning—"My breath is corrupt,
my days are extinct, the graves are ready for me," and
as the preacher commented on the different verses, it was
most interesting to listen to his ability to convert the whole

into a farewell address to his parishioners. He closed by pleading with them to be prepared to answer for the use they had made of his humble ministrations among them, as they would sooner or later have to do before the judgment seat, to which, to all human appearance, he was drawing so near.

The return of the Doctor from the Holy Land was an event looked forward to with the utmost interest by many, and was, in a manner, the inauguration of a new era in his life. His services in the way of lectures, descriptive and amusing, were sought on every hand. He was ready and willing to comply, so far as lay in his power, and many an audience was stirred to interest and excited to laughter by his remarks. His descriptions were frequently so full of wonder that the Doctor was suspected if not of untruth at least of exaggeration. Of this fact he became aware, and on one occasion, when telling the story of the bathing excursion when he lost the covering of his "dome of thought," he made reference to the same. "The shark which pursued me," said he, "had a mouth, ay, nearly as large as a mill door. It seemed satisfied," he continued, "with the wig. It was well for its owner, and though exceedingly sorry over the loss of my wig, I was not less thankful that my head was not inside of it. Now," he added, "you'll be thinking that's a thumper?"

His strange expressions in describing his feelings when ascending the Pyramids, in visiting Jerusalem for the first time, or in lingering by the grave of Jeremiah, were of a kind and character not easily forgotten.

Doctor Aiton had his friends and admirers; he had also (as was to be expected) his detractors. On one occasion, when he had been conducting the service at the funeral of a young man whom he had joined in wedlock only seven weeks before, he was assisted in the same by a young and eloquent clergyman who had newly arrived in the district. Two of the mourners, when on their way to the place of burial, were discussing the powers of the two. "What did ye think o' that young man?" said one; "rather superior to the Doctor yon, I would say."—"Oh no," replied the other; "nae doot it was a very neat and boonie prayer he put up, but ye'll confess the Doctor himsel' was grand.

The young man brought me in mind o' the Kippit Hill—his prayer was sae trim and polished; but the Doctor brought into my mind the Black Mount—bluff and majestic, yet rising high aboon the Kip, trim and bonnie though it be."

In a parish where the Doctor was regular in his appearance in the pulpit on the evening of the Sacramental Sabbath, one old woman there was who had a decided dislike to him, both in regard to his preaching and personal appearance. She had, however, become reconciled very much to him on account of a sermon he had preached on the text—"Who is this that cometh forth as the morning, fair as the moon, clear as the sun, and terrible as an army with banners?" On another similar occasion she was present when he announced as the theme of discourse "The shortness of human life." In the course of his sermon he quoted freely from the book of Job such passages as—"My days are swifter than a weaver's shuttle." He afterwards cited some scenes from the "Vision of Mirza"—"Multitudes were busy in the pursuit of bubbles that glittered in their eyes," &c., &c. His illustrations seemed very homely, and the latent dislike of the old woman was easily rekindled. She quitted the church, saying audibly—"Oh, the rascal! Tae think he could gang up to the poopit and speak aboot bubbles and weavers' shuttles i' the very Sabbath nicht!"

Toward the close of his ministry, the membership of his congregation and general attendance (which, after the Disruption period, had been varied and changeable), showed steady signs of improvement, and, occasionally, on a fine summer Sabbath there was difficulty in finding seats for strangers. Such a state of matters was a cause of much satisfaction to the Doctor, and not unfrequently was the subject of jocular and satirical remarks. One day, when talking over the subject to his precentor, he said he could not understand it, as it was unnatural to suppose that there was any decided improvement in his preaching, at his advanced age. "I sometimes wonder," he said, "if it's not the improved condition of the congregational singing."—"Well," said the precentor, "the Kirk's weel sung."—"It is," replied the Doctor: "I only wish it was as weel preached."

The Doctor's death took place in England, in the house of his daughter and son-in-law, in 1863. His ashes repose on the south and sunny side of the Church, in close proximity to the ashes of Bowie, Gordon, and Donaldson, the Sandilands (father and son), and the other clergymen more or less eminent who were his predecessors, and at no great distance from those of Major Learmonth, laird of Newholm and an elder in Dolphinton, who led the Covenanters at the battle of Rullion Green on that cold and snowy November afternoon so disastrous to the party, when those who fled at the close of the day were scattered over the wild and lonely glens of the Pentlands.

An elegant monument to his memory bears the following inscription :—

"In memory of the Rev. John Aiton, D.D., late minister of this parish, who died at Pyrgo Park, Essex, on the 15th May, 1863, in the 66th year of his age, and 39th of his incumbency, and is buried here, deeply regretted by his flock as their faithful pastor and friend, by his family as a kind and indulgent father." "He being dead yet speaketh."

Since the days of the Doctor the church has been improved and enlarged, an extension being made on the north and dark side. The pulpit has been removed from the west to the south wall, the interior renewed and beautified, while the quaint and characteristic belfry, with the old bell, have been allowed to remain unmolested.

The faces and forms of the clergymen with whom the Doctor's name was so frequently associated have all disappeared from the scene. Mr Paterson of Kirkurd, Mr Alpine of Skirling, Mr Ker of Stobo, Mr Affleck of Lyne, Mr Paul of Broughton, Mr Proudfoot of Culter, Dr Craik of Liberton, Mr M'Lean of Carnwath, and many others, all of whom were intimate friends. Perhaps the latest survivor of a remarkable coterie was the stately and venerable Dr Christison of Biggar. Though we may regard with feelings of satisfaction the more systematic organisation of parochial work in many parishes, the intensified interest in the old sanctuaries of the land, and many other features of improvement, yet we cannot but admit that there existed many excellent qualities of head and heart in the class of men to which we have referred, and which are now but rarely to be found among their successors.

VISITS TO SOME OLD CHURCHYARDS.

TWEEDSMUIR.

"BEAUTIFUL for situation is Mount Zion." Sixty years ago, a person who had all his life travelled in the pursuit of cattle-dealing, was passing the Churchyard of Tweedsmuir, on the outside of the coach, among a group of persons who were discussing the wild grandeur of the scenery through the midst of which they were travelling. "Ay, ay," said the aged person, "I have travelled up and doon Scotland for these last fifty years, but I dinna think I have ever seen a kirk and kirkyaird as bonnilie set as the Kirk an' Kirkyaird o' Tweedsmuir." We are by no means disposed either to question the sincerity or depreciate the taste which led to such an expression, but this we will say, it is a pity that he did not live to more than centenarian age, to look upon the kirk now in its improved appearance, when the model little ecclesiastical edifice, with its graceful and tapering spire, occupies the exact site of the plain, barn-like structure, beneath whose humble roof the honest and peaceful parishioners of Tweedsmuir met for public worship so long. No doubt it had its pleasant memories and hallowed associations to many of those who, 'mid the sacred silence of the Scottish Sabbath, were wont to meet their brethren there, when from the humble belfry went forth the peals that awakened the echoes of the lonely green hills, or who wandered thoughtfully among the rank grass that waved over the graves of those who had shared their joys and sorrows in the comfortable and cheerful homesteads scattered in the glens of the Talla and the Tweed.

It was a bright and beautiful day in June when we first found ourselves wandering in that interesting spot. Fortunately for us, the minister of the parish kindly offered to supply us with any information we might be desirous to obtain, while through his kindness we also obtained admission to the interior of the church, which we scanned with great care and interest. As a whole, the edifice is a credit to the taste and liberality of the parishioners, an ornament to the landscape, and a monument to the good feeling that exists between heritors and people; for though erected at a time when labour was exceedingly high, and in a spot where the most of the materials had to be procured from a great distance, the sum necessary for its erection was raised with little inconvenience, though that sum was by no means inconsiderable. Occupying a commanding site on a triangular promontory, where the Tweed and the Talla mingle their waters, it seems as if the spot had been planned and designed by Nature's hand for the very purpose to which it has been applied; and the order in which it is kept renders it a very pleasant place of retirement. Had we gone there for the purpose of gratifying antiquarian tastes and peculiarities, we would have been disappointed; but being aware that Tweedsmuir was disjoined from Drummelzier about 1643, and erected into a parish about that time, we were convinced that though tradition asserts that the knoll upon which the church is built, with the surrounding enclosure, was formerly the site of a Druidical place of worship, yet certainly not till the date cited would it be used as a place of Christian burial.

We were very much pleased to note on the various stones names of places with which we had been long historically familiar; such as Menzion, Hawkshaw, Fingland, Fruid, Oliver, Earlshaugh, Polmood, Mossfennan, Hearthstane, and Badlieu, and names of persons also, with part of whose family history we were somewhat familiar, such as that of Renwick, Tait, Anderson, Paterson, Welsh, &c., the last having been evidently a prominent name in Tweedsmuir and surrounding parishes. The stones generally are respectable, and substantial more than ornamental; and we could not help thinking that there was a comparative absence of the doggerel epitaphs—so common in many churchyards—which characterised the inscriptions of last century. Some of the epitaphs which we did observe were very interesting. We quote from memory a stanza engraved on a stone which records several deaths, amongst whom are the sire who has reached the years of four-score, and the young maiden cut down in the bloom of youth—

> Death spareth not the aged head,
> Nor manhood fresh and green,
> But blends the locks of eighty-five
> With ringlets of sixteen.

In an unpretentious spot, near the north wall of the Church, we found the burial place of the ministers of the parish, a plain stone marking the grave of the late Mr Tod, the late Mr Gardiner, &c.; though we observed nothing to perpetuate the memory of Mr Wallace, Mr Mushet, or any of the others who held that office last century. Most of them have been men who turned their attention exclusively to their parochial duties—in the words of Gray—

> "Along the cool, sequester'd vale of life
> They kept the noiseless tenor of their way."

Of those of their number who have contributed to the historical reminiscences of the parish, we may mention the Rev. Mr Mushet, who furnished a statistical account of the parish to Sir John Sinclair; and the late Rev. Mr Gardiner, author of a fuller and more extended account, contributed to the *Edinburgh Literary Magazine*; and more recently the Rev. Mr Burns, who was afterwards minister of the Free Church at Corstorphine, who wrote a lengthy and most interesting account of the parish in 1834, for the work then publishing, "Statistical Account of Peeblesshire," by the ministers of the several parishes. One of the principal objects of attraction, however, is the Martyr's Stone. It is a characteristic specimen of many such as are to be found in the churchyards, particularly in the West of Scotland, and among the solitary mountains, or on the lonely moors of our fatherland. This is a matter in which the people of Tweedsmuir have all along taken a great interest; and this spirit has been greatly revived by the enthusiasm of the present minister of the parish, through whose care a small tree, brought from the ruins of the house in which the tragedy took place, now marks the grave and guides the traveller to the spot. As we look upon this matter as attaching an amount of historic interest to the churchyard and parish, we give the inscription in full as we jotted it down for our own satisfaction—"Here lyes John Hunter, martyr, who was cruely murdered at Covehead, by Col. James Douglas and his party, for his adherence to the Word of God and Scotland's covenanted work of reformation, 1685. Erected in the year 1726." On the other side is inscribed the following :—

> When Zion's King was Robbed of his right,
> His witnesses in Scotland put to flight ;
> When popish prelates and Indulgencie
> Combin'd 'gainst Christ to Ruine Presbytrie,
> All who would not unto their idols bow
> They socht them out, and whom they would they slew ;
> For owning of Christ's cause I then did die,
> My blood for vengeance on his enemies did cry.

KAILZIE.

FULLY three miles below the town of Peebles, quite close to the turnpike road leading to Traquair, on a gentle and graceful rising ground, is the old original burying-ground of Kailzie, or, as it was called at a remote period, Hopkellioch. Standing a little removed from the clear rill descending from the heights, and sweeping down the picturesque glen below Laverlaw, and commanding a view of the highly-fertile fields, as well as the majestic hills north of the Tweed, we may safely claim for it a share of that beauty which distinguishes the sites of ecclesiastical edifices of past centuries, more especially, perhaps, in pre-Reformation times,

It was a mild autumn afternoon when we found our way to this peaceful spot, and faintly in the distance could be heard the joke and song from merry youth, busied in securing the precious fruits from the fertile fields on the lands of Kailzie; while on the stately row of trees around us the sere and yellow leaves waited the fitful gale to scatter them once more over the graves of the peaceful and, in many cases, the forgotten dead.

I have often thought there is a very peculiar feeling of interest attaching to these defunct and semi-deserted parochial burying-grounds. One thought that forced itself upon me was the wonderful fact that a parish suppressed

208 years ago should still retain the burying-ground even as it is. Possibly it is partly owing to the fact that it retains the ashes of several of the most extensive and important heritors and landowners within its bounds, such as the family of Horsbrugh of Horsbrugh Castle of that Ilk, the Lairds of Cardrona, &c., the former being long a very important family in the county. A stone in the wall, with a quaint inscription, marks the spot of their sepulture. The middle aisle, which we understand to have been the original burying-place of the Kailzie family, has the following inscription over the doorway :—"It is appointed unto all men once to die, but after death the judgment.—Heb. ix., 27. Oh, that they were wise, that they understood this, that they would consider their latter end.—Deut. xxxii., 29." A burial-place in connection with this estate is now taken up at some distance from the old walls ; and we have reason to believe that, from the warm interest taken in this interesting place of sepulture by the present proprietor, it will not soon be allowed to fall into that state of dilapidation which in other circumstances might have been its lot.

Another thought that rises up is—why did such a parish come to be suppressed ? Time has not established a very sufficient reason for such a transaction; for, at such a distance from any neighbouring parish church, it must have been a great convenience. There was a very considerable congregation in connection with it, and, at least, one hundred communicants, in the year before it was suppressed, and the parishioners, we understand, vigorously opposed its suppression. Were answers to be forthcoming we would be much inclined to put such as the following questions :—"What became of the bell, probably bearing some quaint and suitable inscription, which was wont to awaken the echoes of the lone hills, and summon together the dwellers in those beautiful glens for worship, in a district where so much of the peace and tranquillity of the Sabbath scene reigns even now ?" "What became of the sacred vessels of the little sanctuary, on which they were wont to look, and which they were wont to handle, when met to observe with sincerity and devoutness the love of their dying Lord ?" Such had undoubtedly been valuable relics of interesting times, and pleasant remembrances of parochial history now obsolete. We understand that open-air services are occasionally held here in summer, conducted by the Rev. Mr Wallace, minister of Traquair, within whose parochial boundaries the larger part of the old parish of Kailzie is now included. We are glad to hear of men in his position interesting themselves in these associations; for it is in keeping with the spirit of our times, and a happy and profitable way in which to call to remembrance the former days. Though there is nothing pretentious in the ruins of the old church, as represented in the aisles we have referred to, and, though the number of monumental stones are few, yet some of the more modern are highly creditable, and, withal, the spot is one of much interest. And as in the past there must have been many, so in the present there are still a few, whose thoughts must involuntarily turn to the kirkyard at Kirkburn—dear to them as containing the ashes of loved ones long departed—who there, to use the words of the bard of Lochleven, in the closing lines of his Elegy on Spring:

> "Rest in the hopes of an eternal day
> Till the long night is gone, and the last morn arise."

MUIRKIRK.

TRAVELLING lately to Ayr and the land of Burns, in company with one who had returned to visit the land of his fathers after a residence of forty-five years in Australia, we unexpectedly were compelled to remain over two hours at Muirkirk.

At first sight the difficulty of spending two hours here seemed considerable. Having, however, assured my friend that we were now in the midst of scenes very memorable in Covenanting history, beneath the shadow of Cairntable, and within a few miles of the spot where

> Cameron's sword and his Bible are seen,
> Engrav'd on the stone where the heather grows green,

we could not be altogether wrong in seeking the old church-yard as the likeliest spot to meet with some relic of Covenant times. We had little time to lose, and as little was lost, for within twenty minutes we were wandering within the precincts of "God's Acre,"

> Where heaves the turf in many a mouldering heap.

Our research was very soon crowned with success, for near the upper wall of the burying-ground we espied a small stone, well cared for and preserved, which we regard as one of the best and most characteristic we have ever yet met with. The inscription is as follows:

Here lyes John Smith, who was shot by Col. Buchan and the Laird of Lee, Feb. 1685, for his adherence to the Word of God and Scotland's covenanted work of Reformation. Rev. 12 and 11. Erected in the year 1731.

On the other side is the epitaph—

> When proud apostacy did abjure
> Scotland's Reformation pure,
> And fill'd the land with perjury,
> And all sorts of impurity,
> Such as would not with them comply
> They persecute with hue and cry;
> In the flight was overtaen,
> And for the truth by them was slain.

Tempted by our success we now set out in search lest there might be in the little churchyard of Muirkirk a stone to mark the grave of John Lapraik, the poet, who stood so high in the estimation of Robert Burns, and who died in the parish in the beginning of this century. Again we were successful, and found on a plain tombstone the following inscription:—

In memory of John Lapraik, late of Dalfram, who died at Muirkirk on the 7th May 1807, in the 80th year of his age. Also, his daughter, Jean, who died in 1822, aged 42. And Janet Anderson, his spouse, who died 5 March 1825, aged 85 years.

Before quitting the scene we had a look into the interior of the Parish Church, a substantial and commodious edifice, with fine carved pulpit, and beautifully stained glass windows overhead, the whole of the fittings and furnishings being of the most complete and modern type. The whole

gave proof of the most agreeable relations existing between
heritors and people, and of a warm and consistent interest
in the ordinances of the Church.

Previous to leaving Muirkirk we were fortunate enough
to be introduced to Mr Lapraik, a grandson of the poet, by
whom we were received in the most kindly manner.   He is
a good-looking, elderly gentleman, of over eighty years of
age, and he showed us a copy of Lapraik's poems, now very
rare. My Australian friend thanked him heartily, and
stated that though he had many an interesting interview to
recall when home in the land of his adoption, this was in
all probability the most important of them all; for as the
poetry and songs of Burns were far more prized on distant
shores, so also everything connected with his history became
invested with a greater degree of importance.

We do not for a moment insinuate that we exhausted the
historic resources of Muirkirk Churchyard by our hasty
visit.   There was much to interest and edify, which, because
of the brevity of our time, we left unexplored.

NEWLANDS.

" I COULD willingly close my een in death.   I could frankly
bid fareweel to everything below.   But, oh, I wad like to
be assured that when my departure has ta'en place, my dust
will be laid beside the wife of my youth in the bonny kirkyaird o' the Newlands."   So said an old man, a native of
Peeblesshire, who had long found a home in the north of
Scotland, one with whom the sands of life were ebbing
steadily and fast, and around whose path the shadows of
the long night had begun to gather.

To persons attached to it by associations so tender,
Newlands must seem doubly beautiful, but the spot is one
possessed of many attractive features, and is full of interest
to those who have any taste for the beautiful, though they
may not be bound to it by ties such as are those to
which we have just referred.   The little green plot of
ground lies embosomed in the glebe land, beneath the

shadow of Whiteside Hill, and at a very short distance from the Lyne Water. Here the river glides slowly and peacefully, having arrived at the low-lying haughs where its declivity is almost imperceptible. God's acre is surrounded by the characteristic row of stately and venerable trees, while in the centre rises up the roofless and ivy-covered ruin used for centuries as the place of worship by the parishioners. Appended to, and near, it are the aisles and burying-places of some of the principal heritors and landowners of the past, alternating with the old-fashioned tombstones, and headstones, as well as with the more graceful and artistic memorials of more recent times. Viewed from the gentle rising ground immediately below the bridge, and on the opposite side of the Lyne Water, we can scarcely desire a sight more attractive—more thoroughly illustrative of Scottish rural scenery—or one that is invested with a more decided appearance of perfect repose.

The burying-ground we found to be carefully kept, its condition and appearance being very much above that of some through which it has been our privilege to wander. Having been restored to a decent state of order some years ago, it is now carefully attended to, although it be destitute of much of that ornate and floral work so common in city cemeteries. We may regard this as an improvement, believing as we do that these things are not in harmony with our deep-rooted ideas of the characteristic features of a Scottish kirkyaird.

Within the walls of the old church are interred some of the more enterprising heritors and notable persons of the parish, such as the late Richard Gordon, Esq. of Hallmyre, who during his life-time set such a noble example to the landowners of the district.

A stone in the north wall bears the following inscription : —" To the memory of Alex. Brodie, Esq., author of a history of the Roman Government and other works, who died at Whim House, March 13th, 1858." In another corner are interred the family of Mr Mackintosh of Lamancha, and near by rest the remains of the late Rev. Mr Charteris, in the very spot where he stood when being ordained assistant and successor to the Rev. Charles Findlater, minister of

Newlands, the present commodious place of worship being then only in course of erection. The face and form of Mr Charteris were very interesting and will long be memorable. He frequently appeared at the seasons of communion in the neighbouring parishes, and at the school examinations of auld langsyne the young people hailed his advent with satisfaction and even delight. In his pastoral visitations he was pleasant and kindly, and in every interview with his fellowmen he left the most pleasant impression on the minds of those with whom he came into contact.

The resting-place of Mr Findlater, author of "The Agricultural Survey of Tweeddale," as also of a volume of sermons, is towards the north-east corner of the church-yard, and is marked by a plain unpretentious headstone bearing the following simple inscription:—"Erected in memory of Janet Hay Russell, wife of the Rev. Charles Findlater, minister of this parish; died 2nd August 1828, aged 87, and upon her left of Ann Brown, her cousin-german, who died 9th January 1829, aged 55. In his wife's grave is also deposited the body of the said Rev. Charles Findlater, who was born 10th January 1751, was minister of Linton from 1777 till 1790, and of Newlands till his death on the 29th May 1838." Mr Findlater was not prominent as a cleric, but as a kind, philanthropic gentleman. As an agriculturist whose opinion was highly valued, he has added considerably to the literature of the county, and his name will always be cherished as that of one of the worthies of Tweeddale.

We found, in one corner, a stone marking the burial-place of the relatives of Dr Craig, formerly minister of the Relief Church of Newlands; and, in another, one marking that of the family of the Rev. Mr Rutherford, present minister at Mountaincross. Only one other stone records the life and labours of former ministers of the parish, viz., that to the memory of Stephen Paton, who died in 1755. No trace of anything could we find to the memories of Mr Moffat, or Mr Dickson, or the Rev. Patrick Purdie, though we understand an inscription on a very old stone gives the name of the last mentioned.

The date on the old church, 1725, has evidently been recorded at a time when the edifice was undergoing alterations, as there is an arched doorway near the west end, and a very interesting Gothic window in the east gable, which point to a period centuries prior to the date referred to. "This window," says Mr Findlater in the Statistical Account of Peeblesshire published in 1834, "has now been converted into a door leading to a gallery." We are informed this was in the time that Lord Chief-Baron Montgomery occupied the mansion-house of Whim. James Montgomery, to whom we refer, was afterwards Baronet of Stanhope, and was undoubtedly one of the most notable men of whom Newlands could boast. He was one of the more eminent men who have arisen in the county of Tweeddale, being also the first Scotchman who attained to the position of Chief-Baron of His Majesty's Exchequer in Scotland.

At no great distance from the old church is the grave of Robert Howlieson, the centenarian, a very plain stone marking the place of his interment. We have often been privileged to sit by his fireside to enjoy his jokes and listen to his old-world stories; and when he was presented with a purse of sovereigns, and an address of congratulation on his entering his 103rd year, we listened to the brief reply tendered by him. In the near neighbourhood we found the graves of three young persons, all members of one family, that had suffered from the ravages of consumption and fever, bringing forcibly to our mind the passage of Scripture—"The old and the young go down to the grave together." In the same division of the churchyard rests one who was long and well known in the district as a mechanical genius of a high order, Alex. Cuthbertson, watchmaker. His grave is marked by a suitable and interesting memorial erected to him by an old friend, one of the most distinguished men of his day, and one of the most enterprising heritors of the parish.

The names of the leading agriculturists of the past are well represented on the various headstones and monuments, and during the brief hour we spent there we came upon the names and the resting-places of many amiable persons whose friendship we long ago had enjoyed and prized, men who had long been well known and much respected in the district. The newest grave in the ground was that of William Welsh, a local poet and author, who took a warm interest in the history of the district, and who could communicate much interesting and valuable information on local subjects.

There is in this churchyard a notable scarcity of epitaphs in rhyme, such are to be found in most of the old parochial burying-grounds.   More frequently the names of individuals with the date of their death is followed by some suitable and well chosen passage of Scripture, such as at the graves of the Jacksons of Altarstone, " The gift of God is eternal life," &c., &c., while some of those belonging to the class to which we have just referred are rather worthy of notice. The following is given on a stone to a family of the name of Kay of Leadburn, referring to a young girl eleven years of age :—

> The lovely bud so young and fair,
>   Called hence by early doom,
> Just came to show how sweet a flower
>   In paradise would bloom.

In another part we found a stone with the lines—

> Oh, trust not to your fleeting breath,
>   Nor call the time your own,
> Around you see the scythe of death
>   Is mowing thousands down.

The last we took note of was the inscription on a stone erected to a Mr Borrowman, teacher in Kilbucho, and his sister :—" They lived respected, died deeply regretted, and the friends whom they loved, Jacob-like, carried back their bones into their native Canaan, and raised this memento over them."

DUNSYRE.

In a lonely trackless region, on a far-off foreign shore,
I am feeling, ah, I own it, that life's journey 's nearly o'er;
I have struggled on for riches, I have got me wealth and gold,
Yet the pleasure that they bring me is a tale that soon is told,
And within my weary bosom nought so strong as the desire

To be laid beside my fathers in the kirkyard of Dunsyre;
Yet the wish is worse than fruitless, and the dream is very vain,
For the ocean ne'er shall bear me to my own dear land again.

THE foregoing lines are said to have been penned by a
native of this parish, and that very shortly before his death.
The ties that bound him to this little burial-place were of a
type more sacred than the tastes that led us to visit the
same, and yet we felt it to be the realisation of a long
cherished hope when we found ourselves at liberty to spend
an hour there in quietude and calm composure. In a parish
so rich in Covenant associations, we naturally expected to
find some interesting memorials of men belonging to or
connected with the parish, who figured in the history of
those troublous times. In this, however, we were disappointed; for though James Baillie of Todholes was one
of those who suffered for their devotion to the Covenanting
cause, we found no trace of his family, or any tombstone to
James Hamilton, laird of Anston, who in 1667 was apprehended and imprisoned by order of the Privy Council on
suspicion of his having given shelter to his son-in-law, Major
Learmonth of Newholm, after the battle of the Pentlands.
Neither, we presume, is there any stone to tell of the family
of the Rev. W. Veitch, tenant of the farm of Westhills,
afterwards minister of Peebles, and of St. Michael's,
Dumfries. Possibly, however, there may have been inscriptions to the memory of some of the aforesaid on some of
the old heavy throughstones, where there is now no vestige
remaining either of inscription or ornament. Red freestone,
probably brought down from Easton moor, or some of the
hilly parts of the parish, having been used—stones of a
particular kind, that throw off scales from time to time—
every thing is obliterated. In some cases, to judge from
their situation, these stones must have been erected to
ministers of the parish. One of these is spoken of as, "The
stane to the last curate." The last curate was Robert
Skein, who left the parish at the Revolution, and died in
Edinburgh in 1721, but that he was buried here is somewhat
doubtful. A large flat stone marks the grave of Henry
Duncan, the first minister after the Revolution. A plain
marble slab in the church wall records the ministry of the

Rev. Mr Bradfute, who was succeeded by his son. A plain headstone marks the grave of the Rev. William Meek, the author of several prose and poetical works. In the west corner of the ground we were gratified by seeing a fine headstone over the grave of one whom we knew well, viz., Martin Porteous, for a long period parochial schoolmaster, a man of superior intelligence and refined literary tastes. Among other interesting relics we were delighted to see a headstone marking the graves of the Watsons of Weston, father and grandfather of the late Jean L. Watson, authoress of "Bygone Days in our Village," and other valuable works, thus pleasantly forming a connecting link between Peebles-shire and Dunsyre. One near to it gives a genealogical register of the "Browns of Dunsyremains," and their very ancient connection with the parish, while near to these are several very old unreadable stones, whose quaint insignia reminds us of the words of Gray—

"With uncouth rhymes and shapeless sculpture decked."

The quaint little church, which has of late been restored at a considerable expense, is of the Pre-Reformation style, and its restoration has been accomplished in the best taste. With its modest tower rising from the picturesque knoll we regard Dunsyre as one of the finest ideals of such a parish as that where Gray penned that "Elegy" which remains an ornament to the century in which it was written, and must live as long as the language honoured with its record.

SKIRLING.

IN paying a visit to this ancient burial-place we find ourselves within the precincts of the churchyard of one of the quietest parishes, and one of the most beautiful districts in the south of Scotland. Viewed from the picturesque knoll where the church stands, and beneath the bright sunshine of a July day, with the fertile crofts and well-kept cottages nestling between the uplands to the north and

south, we venture to say a more peaceful rural picture is
rarely to be found. We do not wonder that this parish
should have been the birthplace and cradle of one of those
artists of whom Scotland has reason to be proud, and on
whose account principally we sought the silence of the
picturesque scene where

"The rude forefathers of the hamlet sleep,"

and it was with little trouble that we discovered the decent
memorial to James Howe, son of the Rev. Mr Howe, minister
of this parish. The stone bears the following suitable
inscriptions :—

Here rest the remains of James Howe, artist, son of the Rev.
William Howe, minister of Skirling. Born 30th August 1780;
died 14th July 1836.

He who could make with life the canvas glow,
    In death's deep slumber lies this turf below,
But Death, who triumphs o'er the mouldering frame,
    Dims not the lustre of the artist's fame.
        Erected by his admirers in his native parish.

In our search after old stones, we were somewhat disappointed. There are a few, but we could decipher none
older than that of Beatrice, relict of Patrick Crighton, who
died in March 1696. There are to be found several interesting specimens of those rhyming epitaphs, where the dead
find words wherewith to address the living, and from which
we quote the following :—

My grave is witness to the power of death,
My corpse enclosed is foyld of vital breath,
But yet the glorious and almighty King,
In death slew death that I may victoriously sing.

Another over the grave of two children reads—

In life's gay spring we bid this world adieu,
And leave all fleeting joys and cares to you.

The numerous respectable obelisks and headstones, with
the prominent number of Nobles, Watsons, Clarks, Proud-

foots, Threeplands, &c., with their kindly and affectionate language, speaks well for the intelligence, morality, and piety of the people of the district; and in our scrutiny we observed several names which awoke remembrances of friendships of the remote past, as well as others that spoke to us of those of the present day. In one particular corner of the burial ground were several large "throughstanes" that recorded the names and enumerated the virtues of successive clergymen who had ministered to the people of Skirling. In a pleasant spot is a stone erected over the grave of a child by the Rev. Dr Hanna, who was minister of the parish during the days of the Disruption. Though church disputes form no part of our enquiries, we cannot but be reminded of the fact that Skirling stood out conspicuously in these times, and that nearly the whole congregation followed their eminent pastor when he withdrew from the Establishment. The Free Church is now well supported in the district, but a goodly congregation gathers in the Parish Church of Skirling, and a member of a family belonging to the same was lately elected to be the successor of a clergyman in the north, who has long been acknowledged as one of the leading thinkers of the present day. In our conversation with the villagers we found that the memory of Howe, the "animal painter" as he is termed, is fresh among the older people; and in different homes we were shewn a few of his productions, all of a very interesting type. One of the families to which we refer is that of the Proudfoots, brothers of the late Rev. Mr Proudfoot of Culter, a man whose name is well known in literary circles, a poet of considerable note, and withal a son of whom Skirling has just reason to be proud. Fifty years ago the village was famous on account of its fairs, which, however, have long ago been removed to Biggar. As for the feudal family of "The Cockburns," who for nearly three centuries held undisputed possession, there is nothing left with which their name is identified, and of their residence—the "Castle of Skirling"—all that can be seen of it is the spot where it stood, the lands and surroundings being now carefully and successfully cultivated by an industrious and intelligent peasantry.

NEWHALL.

WE have made choice of the above subject, not because we can establish for it any claim to be a remnant of any old ecclesiastical burying-ground (though in close proximity to the fragment of the old ruin known as "The Chapel"), but simply because of the quaintness and the beauty of its situation, and its close relation to the scenery of "The Gentle Shepherd." It is also the resting-place of the Browns of Newhall, whose name invariably gives rise to memories of the most agreeable character, and which has for nearly a century been familiar as a household word in the homes nestling in the bosom of the Pentlands. We have often at a distance surveyed this peaceful place of sepulture, when on a bright summer day Habbie's Howe was full of visitors and excursionists, and the sounds of music and of merriment resounded through the picturesque glen; but on this occasion we chose the quietude of a dull December day, when no sound broke the silence save the gentle murmur of the Esk's blue waters wimpling down the classic vale. We first scanned the quaintly carved old stone, which has often been eagerly surveyed by many who have long ago quitted this earthly scene. It bears the following simple inscription, so tenderly expressive of warm parental affection:—"This head-stone marks the remains of Thomas Dunsmore Brown, an uncommon fine child, who was born on the 5th April, 1807, and after an illness of only eight hours, died in Newhall House, 19th September, 1808.—R.B." On the other side are the lines:

> Alas, young tenant of the tomb,
> In vain to thee shall spring return,
> Though all her sweets around thee bloom,
> They cannot cheer thy clay-cold urn.
>
> Where's now the bloom that on thy cheek
> Vied with the rose's vermile dye?
> Thy tongue how mute that prattled sweet,
> How dark thy once bright beaming eye.
>
> Deep is thy slumber, lovely shade!
> No plaint of woe can reach thine ear;
> Where thou in earth's cold bosom laid
> No more shalt see soft pity's tear.

The foregoing lines are from a poem on the subject by James Forrest, weaver in Carlops; a local poet of considerable note, a man of refined literary tastes, and an intimate friend of the then Laird of Newhall, who bemoaned the loss of the child.   The lines were wont to be repeated long ago and oft by many a schoolboy, and referred to as "the bonnie metre on the headstane at Newha'."   Another stone, evidently recently erected, records the decease of Harriet Brown, who died in 1882, and her youngest sister, Charlotte, who died at Edinburgh in 1835, the latter being still often spoken of in affectionate terms by older people in the district as "Laird Brown's nice lassie that dee'd young." A third headstone records the death of the first Brown of Newhall, a man of great enterprise, who, through a long life, made every endeavour to establish the fact of Newhall estate being the genuine scenery of "The Gentle Shepherd" of Allan Ramsay.   He also spent much time and money in beautifying the valley, and in opening those walks which have for fourscore years been such a boon to the public, and especially to the citizens of Edinburgh. This privilege was kindly continued by the late Mr Hugh H. Brown, who died fully twenty years ago, and is still continued, and very greatly taken advantage of. The stone referred to bears the following inscription :— "Sacred to the beloved memory of Robert Brown, Esq. of Newhall and Carlops, who died in Newhall House, 27th December, 1832 ; and of Elizabeth Kerr, his wife, who died in Newhall House, May 1828.   'He that believeth in the Son hath everlasting life.'"   So, within a short distance of the fairy den, almost within view of the quaint and interesting mansion, near to Mary's Bower, and overhanging the Esk, slumber the ashes of one to whom the beauty of the surrounding scenery was very patent and very enjoyable, as also of one whose form and face were familiar to us in childhood, and of whose uprightness and geniality many can testify, who now find it a pleasure to recall the memory of him whose end was peaceful as his life had been.

REMINISCENCES OF NOTABLE CHARACTERS
CONNECTED WITH CARLOPS.

IN attempting to give some reminiscences of notable and eccentric characters connected with the village and district of Carlops, one feels considerably at a loss, not for want, but rather from a super-abundance of material; for even within the somewhat limited period of our remembrance, there was to be found in this district as rich and as interesting a variety of the various types of Scottish character as perhaps could be found in any district in Scotland.

We would refer in these reminiscences to Mr GEORGE HUNTER, who so long taught the little school at Nine-Mile-Burn, to which he travelled daily from Carlops. Mr Hunter was from his youth a cripple, and we can believe that it was shyness and modesty on account of this infirmity which prevented him from pushing himself forward into some situation of greater importance, for which he was well-qualified. As an arithmetician he was rarely excelled, and his penmanship was remarkably beautiful, as can be proved by many specimens preserved among the farmers in the surrounding district. As a land surveyor his services were frequently called into requisition, and it is worthy of note that he had much to do with the division and sub-division of Slipperfield Moor, when the farms of Felton, Hyndford, Mendick, and Medwynmains were laid off, a few years after the new turnpike road had been made. In consequence of his lameness, all his labours had to be prosecuted on horseback; yet this was to him little hindrance, and more than once he, by this means, climbed the steep sides of Mendick.

The emoluments from the school, taught by him for a period of nearly forty years, were not large, and consisted of the fees, with a small supplementary salary from Mr Brown of Newhall and a few others, who took a considerable interest in the educational affairs of the district.   Now, under the roof of a commodious and handsome edifice, the children of the locality enjoy all the benefits of a well-equipped Public School.   Mr Hunter lived to an old age, and retained his mental faculties to the last.   The evening of his days was, however, clouded by trial and bereavement. The name of the family is not now known in the district, and the ashes of one who sent many an active man and excellent scholar into the world, slumber unnoticed in an obscure corner of the old churchyard of Linton.

We cannot here omit to mention the name of WILLIE LEWIS, grocer and weaver, whose jokes Mr Hunter enjoyed to the full.   It was customary for people in business in Carlops to have some representation on their sign-boards identifying the village with the scenes of " The Gentle Shepherd."   Willie Lewis was no exception in this respect, for in the centre of his sign-board was the intimation, " William Lewis, grocer," while on one corner was a painting representing " Mause, the witch," and on the other a figure representing " Bauldy."   Underneath all were these words from " The Gentle Shepherd "—

> "An' yonder's Mause; ay, ay, she kens fu' weel
> When ane like me comes rinnin' to the deil."

William's witty replies and quaint remarks were subjects of conversation with the villagers of Carlops; so much so indeed, that not unfrequently they developed into bye-words and proverbs, which are still used in the locality with the use and wont introduction—" As Willie Lewis used to say." Willie was a regular attender at the Secession meeting-house in Linton, and an attentive listener to the lengthy lectures and sermons delivered there; while his lank, spare form, with the plaid carelessly hung over his shoulders, is still fresh in the memory of many.   On special occasions, and in regard to special preachers, his estimate was generally pretty correct, though from the humorous terms in which his opinions were couched, there was frequently a difficulty in preserving becoming gravity among those who were both eager and curious to hear his sentiments.

Neither dare we pass over the names of JOHNNY TAMSON and ROBBY CAIRNS. The former was for a very long time a truly public man in the village. At an earlier period he was agent for the weavers, and was the owner of a large shop; while he also had a grocer's shop and kept a little public-house, familiarly known by the appellation of "The Elder's," he being a member of Linton Kirk-Session for little short of half a century. Kind and obliging, and very courteous, John Thomson was a great favourite in the locality. A native of the quaint village of Douglas, where his father officiated as beadle in the Parish Church, John had many interesting reminiscences of this place to tell, but there was one more than any other which he took great pleasure in repeating. It was a scene at a Douglas Fair, and occurred when he was a lad of thirteen years of age. On the occasion referred to he was being led by his father through the various sights of interest in the Fair, and latterly found himself among a group of persons witnessing an engagement at putting the ball, when one who distinguished himself at this trial of strength was Robert Burns, the Ayrshire ploughman. The parties afterwards adjourned to an inn, where John and his father formed part of the company. There was present among them a farmer named Gilbertfield, who was a little noisy and stood in the way of the company's enjoyment by continually speaking of his "kye and sheep." To rid the company of a comparative nuisance, Burns stated that if Gilbertfield would leave the room for twenty minutes he would have his epitaph written when he came back. Gilbertfield quitted the company, but returned at the prescribed time and demanded the fulfilment of the promise. "Well," said Burns, "I have not got it written down, but it is something like the following—

> Here Gilbertfield, droll honest chield,
> Aneath this stane does sleep,
> Oh were it given for him in heaven
> To deal in kye and sheep."

Robert Cairns, to whom we have already referred, was long engaged as a freestone quarryman at Deepsykehead, yet amidst a life of constant and heavy labour he found time in his leisure hours to improve his mind, and also to engage in such recreative work as bird-stuffing, for which he was well known. He had few opportunities of mixing with those who were socially or intellectually his superiors, but on one occasion he enjoyed an interview with Sir Walter Scott, of which he was wont to speak with great zest. He was, along with his future wife, Peggy Tait, calling at the mansion on one of the domestics, and on quitting it he was accosted by Sir Walter, who was loitering about the pleasure grounds, when the following brief conversation ensued:—

Sir Walter—And so you have been paying a visit to one of my domestics?

Robert—Yes, sir.

Sir Walter—I hope she has had leisure to converse with you.

Robert—Oh, yes.

Sir Walter—I can hear you do not belong to this locality.

Robert—No, sir. I am a native of and a residenter in Peeblesshire.

Sir Walter—Oh, yes, and in what part of Peeblesshire do you reside?

Robert—In the village of Carlops, and parish of Linton.

Sir Walter—Oh, indeed! How is Mr Forrester? (referring to the father of the present minister of the parish.)

Robert—He is quite well.

Sir Walter—Always able to discharge pulpit duty I suppose?

Robert—Oh, yes, he was at his post on Sabbath last.

Sir Walter—And Mr Goldie and Mr Ferrier, you will know them? (referring to two important heritors of the parish, both of whom were connected with the law.)

Robert—Oh, yes, I know them by sight, but moving in a sphere of life different from mine, I cannot boast of any acquaintance with them.

Sir Walter laughed heartily, and bidding him good-bye, Robert expressed the hope that he had not made a bogle of the Baronet.

A person of very peculiar personal appearance—long a tenant of and dweller at Kittleyknowe, near Carlops—was JAMIE HORSBURGH, whose form was well known among the worshippers in Linton Meeting-house, with which he had been in connection from his youth.   James was a well-read intelligent man, but was subject to visitations of mental aberration, and when under these he generally strolled about in an unsettled state, both late and early.   Frequently at an early hour, on a bright summer or autumn morning, were the echoes of Habbie's Howe, and the very woods of Newhall awakened by James lilting over "Tibby Fowler o' the glen," or some other favourite old Scotch song.   James was a skilled theologian, and was much enamoured with the eloquence of Mr Renwick, who was minister of the Secession body in Linton from 1811 till 1829. Mr Renwick sometimes conducted open-air meetings at Harbour Craig, and as James was in the habit of composing verses, we need not wonder that he celebrated the place and the occasion in a short poem to which the following is the introduction:—

Here in this low sequester'd glen,
Stands Harbour Craig, an ancient rock,
A safe retreat in days of old
From persecution's cruel stroke.

Here our forefathers oft did meet
To hear the glorious gospel preached,
And from this place, to us, their sons,
The Word of God is clearly teached.

For Mr Renwick has preached here
These four years past with great applause,
Bold and courageous, without fear,
Undaunted in his Master's cause.

A friend of his had, by a second marriage, lost the society and esteem of one who by his first marriage was his brother-in-law, and the following verse gives Jamie's comment on the circumstance—

How fleeting is relationship
    When friendship is not there;
'Tis like a spark upon the deep,
    Or a bubble full of air.
It soon explodes and vanishes,
    And passes out of sight;
'Tis like a fiery meteor,
    Or vision of the night.

On one occasion he was animated by a little jealousy when informed that Crichton, the weaver, had begun verse-making, and had written on different subjects of local interest.   James gave vent to his feelings in the following stanza—

> John Crichton 's but a babblin' fool
>   Compared wi' men o' learnin';
> A silly coof, a cool-the-loom—
>   Sae, lassies, a' tak' warnin'.

One day when crossing thro' Habbie's Howe he saw Laird Brown approaching, when suddenly he took his hat off, set it down on the ground, and stepped into it with his feet; whereupon Mr Brown asked him in a jocular and kindly manner what he meant by such a performance? Jamie replied, " Weel, Mr Brown, the last time I met ye, ye complained that I had not greeted ye wi' my ordinary salute, so the day I thocht I wad mak' amends for a faut."

On a green haugh a little below the foot of Habbie's Howe, and near to where the classic Esk bids farewell to a variety of scenery almost unsurpassed in beauty, to wind through the wild and romantic tract that intervenes till it enters the policies of Penicuik House, stands the ruins of a little cottage and a few out-houses, known for long as the Bleach-field, and for one half-century, at least, associated with the name of JOHN WATSON. In his early days, John, while engaged as a weaver, acquired a taste for reading, which kept a firm hold of him, even when he gave up this profession and betook himself to out-door labour.   Indeed, through the whole course of a long life, he found his chief pleasure in his books; and not only so, but he gave proof of a very refined and superior taste in literary pursuits. Being gifted with a most retentive memory, he could, with the greatest ease, cite lengthy passages from his favourite poets, and blank verse was as familiar to him in the latter years of his life as if he were actually reading from the authors he delighted to quote. John's humble domicile was resorted to by many who could enjoy and appreciate his intellectual superiority and his ready wit, of the latter of which qualities we give a few specimens.

One fine summer day he was visited by his landlord, Hugh H. Brown, Esq. of Newhall, who, while conversing with him, observed lying in the end window a copy of a volume of poems, published by his father, the previous proprietor of Newhall, who distributed copies of the same among his tenantry and friends. The Laird, as John invariably termed him, thinking this an excellent opportunity of smelling his breath on the subject, asked him, "Now, John, you that can test the worth or worthlessness of such a publication, what do you think of these pieces of my father's?" "Weel, Mr Broon, that's just a question I wad rather no answer," replied John Watson. "Nonsense," rejoined the Laird; "let me hear your opinion of them. I know you to be an honest man, and also an acknowledged judge of such matters, and be your answer what it may, it will give no offence."—"Weel, Mr Broon, I am truly sorry to be compelled to state that the maist I can say for them is that 'they are perfect trash.'" On one occasion when calling on an old friend, a merchant in a neighbouring village, to see the new premises erected by him, as also a new dwelling-house, &c., John quietly surveyed the whole without making any remark. Before leaving, however, his friend, while treating John to some refreshment, said— "But, John, ye've never said a word as to what ye think o' my improvements. What are you gaun to say about them?" —"Oh, what am I gaun to say," said John, with a sly, characteristic twitch of his eye, "What can I say but just what the Queen o' Sheba said when she visited Solomon and reviewed a' his grandeur—'The half hath not been told me.'"

"Ye used to be very fond of Dr Young, uncle," said his nephew, who, when calling upon him one day, found him pondering over "Milton's Paradise Lost."—"Ah," replied he, "that is true, an' I'm fond o' him yet. Nae doot," continued John, "to appreciate Dr Young, ane maun be in a certain frame o' mind ; but on a lang winter nicht, when I'm in ane o' my thochtfu' moods, I wadna gi'e the fellowship o' the seraphic author o' the Nicht Thochts for a' the 'gold o' Peru.'"

"D'ye no think," said a neighbour to him for the sake of a joke, "that Dr Skae has maybe some particular reason for ca'in' on ye sae often?" John, who was never to be found from home, quaintly replied, "There's nae doot lunacy shows itsel' in mony a divers phase, an' developes itsel' in mony a different form, an' if there's ae man that kens that better than anither, it's my learned friend Dr Skae, wha's aye a welcome guest at my fireside as often as he likes to ca'. Be his object what it may, we crack thegither weel."

One stormy winter night, when a number of his friends were seated around his cheerful hearth, the conversation turned upon Tennyson, at that period less known to the world than now. John had read his first performances with a little indifference, but after having perused some of his subsequent productions he formed a very decided opinion of them. When the matter was then brought up, John, with his usual enthusiasm, raised his hand and exclaimed, "Depend upon this, Tennyson will by-and-by, mak' room for hissel' amang the michty and the great, or I'm nae judge o' poetry. But," he continued, "there's in the present day a tendency to overlook the merits o' ane wha has a far mair decided claim on our admiration than ony poet that has ever written, for never did poet gi'e expression to the loves and the fears, the joys and sorrows of his countrymen, as the Immortal Burns has dune, and never was a more faithful eulogium pronounced on him than that gi'en in the words of the American poet, Halleck, when he said of him—

> ' His is that language of the heart,
>   To which the answering heart can speak;
> Thought, word, that bids the warm tear start;
>   Or the smile light the cheek.
>
> And his that music, to whose tone
>   The common pulse of man keeps time,
> In cot or castle's mirth or moan,
>   In cold or sunny clime.'

An' on a nicht like this, when Boreas hurls his tempests frae the angry north, where'll ye find language sae suitable as his ain, when in ane o' his finest epistles he says—

> ' Oh, Nature, a' thy shows and forms
> For feeling, pensive, hearts hae charms,
> Whether the simmer kindly warms
>   Wi' life and licht,
> Or winter howls wi' gusty storms
>   The lang dark nicht.' "

In politics John was a decided Liberal, and took a very prominent part in the conversations and debates that arose in the convivial circles which were gathered together from time to time in the public-house kept in Carlops by John Thomson, and in that at the Nine-Mile-Burn, then kept by John Robb. Often did the little alehouse resound with roars of laughter, at the humorous and quaint remarks made by him, and the many laughable anecdotes which he delighted to tell. In him also the tales and legends of the district found a safe repository, and he could clothe them in language well calculated to leave a lasting impression on the minds of the young, who delighted to gather round him, and to whom he was always prepared to show the greatest indulgence. With him, however, much of the past history of the district has been for ever lost sight of, for John Watson had a great indifference to committing his ideas to manuscript, though, sometimes, his family were successful in persuading him to do so.

Thirty years ago, John was in Linton at a funeral, and standing alone gazing round him in the churchyard, he was accosted by a friend, "John, ye'll nae doot be thinking this is an unco ill keepit place?"—"I'm no thinking ony sic thing," he replied, "I prefer this to ye're fine cemeteries wi' their ornaments and flummeries. I've aye the idea they scarcely become the resting-place of the dead. A plain country kirkyaird like this invariably reminds me of the beautiful elegy written by Gray; and a deserted corner like that," continued he, pointing to a place where hemlock and nettles were rankling in abundance, "reminds me mair particularly o' the verse of his in which he says—

> ' Perhaps in this neglected spot is laid
> Some heart once pregnant with celestial fire;
> Hands that the rod of empires might have sway'd,
> Or wak'd to ecstacy the living lyre.' "

Ere one short year had elapsed from the time of which we have spoken, John Watson had passed away, and his ashes had been laid to rest within a few yards of the spot where this conversation took place. On the forenoon of a sultry summer Sabbath, a very large and respectable company of mourners followed his remains to the grave, and the writer can remember of not a few superior men worshipping in the Parish Church of Linton on that day, several of whom had come from a long distance to pay the last tribute of respect to his memory.

In the district of which we have already been speaking, there was no name more familiar to the inhabitants (for half a century) than that of TAMMAS TAMSON, the joiner o' Nine-mile-burn; a plain, plodding, honest man. Possessed of a good deal of common sense, kindly and obliging among his neighbours, and an elder o' the kirk, there was no person whose advice was more frequently sought, or more highly prized than was Tammas Tamson. In his conversation with his fellow-men, there was, however, one phrase of which he so regularly made use, that in the latter years of his life he was quite as well known by this as by his own name. For instance, when asked by any friend in difficulty as to how he should act in certain circumstances in which he had been or was likely to be placed, the reply of Tammas Tamson was invariably prefaced with these words—"With respect unto that." If informed of any sudden death—"With respect unto that, it's a very lood warnin' for us a' to be ready"; or had some well-doing, faithful wife been deprived of her husband—"With respect unto that, it's a very trying bereavement"; or had some amiable young woman gone astray from the paths of virtue—"With respect unto that, we may weel pity baith the puir lassie and her heart-broken parents." If invited to a wedding, a kirn, or a merry-making of any sort— "With respect unto that, I'll be very glad to be there, if health be granted till that time."

The attainments of Tammas, as a joiner, were well known to be very moderate. On one occasion, when making a case for an eight-day clock, it was found that the wood frame round the dial projected rather seriously over the

L

figures. The good wife on looking at it said, "But have a care o' me, Tammas; ye hae sae little glass in 't that it 's hardly possible to ken what o'clock it 's, the frame comes oot owre the chapters a' thegither."—"O weel," replied Tammas, "the pane is sma', but with respect unto that, ye can hae a guid guess as it is; and when ye want to ken exactly, why, with respect unto that, ye 've nae mair to do than open the door and see for yersel'."

One day, when engaged in thrashing his corn in his low-roofed barn, a friend called, and after gazing for a few minutes at Tammas as he skillfully wielded the flail, he expressed his astonishment that the weapon never came in contact with his head. Tammas replied : "With respect unto that, I 've just to exercise the same spirit o' watchfulness that 's needed in the midst o' mair serious difficulties, and in the face o' greater dangers, as we fecht the battle o' life."

Weaver Hope of Monkshaugh (the original name of Bleachfield), who was strongly suspected of smuggling, in the secluded glen where he dwelt, was himself a character; and when about to leave his little croft, he was puzzled at the idea of removing his furniture, especially his wooden beds, lest the roof might fall in, and the whole tenement become a ruin, while he in terms of his lease was bound to leave it in habitable repair as he had entered thereupon. Disclosing his difficulties to John Cairns o' the *Steele*, the latter proposed that he should invite to his domicile honest Tammas Tamson, treating him to a drap o' the best, a commodity which Weaver Hope seldom lacked. "I 'll be doon to meet him," and, added John, "With respect unto that, I 've nae doot Tammas will put the whole matter right." The proposal commended itself · at once, the night was fixed, and Tammas Tamson was invited. The evening came, and the company was simply a meeting of worthies. After all had partaken freely of the Athole brose, and had their conversational powers quickened, Weaver Hope took the opportunity of explaining to Tammas the position in which he was placed, and expressed the hope, that as a practical man, he would be able to help him out of his difficulty by certifying to Laird Brown that the dwelling was in tolerable habitable repair as it was when he took possession.

Without quitting the easy chair, Tammas took a hasty survey of the joisting overhead, and of the tenement at large, and said, "With respect unto that, I think I'll have no difficulty whatsomever in satisfying the laird on that point." The company cheered the old joiner, and Johnnie Cairns slyly remarked, it was a question he had often put to himsel', "What wad the district be without a man like Tammas Tamson?"

Within a few weeks of this meeting, Weaver Hope left Monkshaugh, and only three days had elapsed when the roof fell in. The removal of the two box beds was more than it could afford, and the formerly snug little cottage stood a roofless ruin. Tammas Tamson was sent for by the laird, who expressed his astonishment that a man in whom every body confided should have been guilty of such misrepresentation. In his indignation at the whole matter, he insinuated that the joiner could not but know that such a collapse was likely to take place, to which Tammas replied, "With respect unto that, Mr Brown, there was no appearances to indicate such a disaster on the nicht I made the inspection, I can assure ye."

One night near the close of his days, a friend, who called at his dwelling to share his conversation for a few hours, found him seated at his supper. His humble board was crowned with no dainties, the plain plate of "porridge" (at that time the customary evening meal) was all that was set before him. At that period, fully 50 years ago, the harvests were very precarious. The oats frequently were ill got, and the consequence was that when brought home from the mill, the meal had a loathsome appearance, and gave forth a fusty flavour. Of the worst type seemed the evening meal of the aged joiner. "Your oatmeal's like my ain, Tammas; it's surely no great."—"It is not," he replied; "in fact, I scarcely ever had it waur."—"I wonder very much," continued his friend, "that ye can mak' a supper o't."—"A supper o't," said Tammas; "with respect unto that, I'm as happy owre my humble meltith as the king can be wi' a' his dainties."

CHARLES WILSON.

WE have already referred to the interesting variety of individuality to be met with in the locality of Carlops, we will now confine our remarks to one who did not seek to distinguish himself as a politician, and who professed nothing more than a moderate taste for, and appreciation of, poetry. He, however, found scope for the development of his artistic powers, and devoted his leisure hours to carving in stone, and in investing with a remarkable beauty the cottage and garden which he occupied. These are situated at the south-west extremity of the village of Carlops, on the banks of the clear little stream emerging from the wild and picturesque glen stretching along the base of Stoneypath Hill and Carlops Hill, and which, after winding down by Pyet Hall, Lanelybield, and Kittleybridge, joins the Esk at the foot of Habbie's Howe. We refer to Charles Wilson, plasterer, who, though not a native of the parish of West Linton, came to it at a very early age, and spent a long life in the district. From early years he evinced a keen appreciation of sculpture, and the devotion of his spare hours to it was not only the outcome of his taste, but to him a scource of great enjoyment. After his collection had increased considerably, he contemplated the erection of a little temple or grotto in his picturesque garden, and commenced his preparations with great alacrity and enthusiasm. The only spot available was found to be exceedingly soft, and, much to his discomfort, he was informed by some of the old residenters that it had at one time been a linthole or a stagnant pool beside a running stream, such as were often used long ago for steeping lint. Determined, however, not to be overcome, he set to work, and had a secure foundation made by the driving in of heavy wooden piles. He thereafter proceeded with his quaint little erection in which he hoped to store the smaller productions of his own hands, and which he accordingly did.

As a further proof of the indomitable perseverance which characterised Mr Wilson, we may mention that the large red freestone from which he wrought the figure of the lion which rested over the antique portico (an object of great curiosity to many a passer-by, contented with a peep from the bridge, and never privileged further to investigate the museum of curiosities), was brought from the Cairn Hill, and every one who knows how inaccessible such a locality is will have an idea of the labour thereby incurred.

The residence of Charles Wilson was visited by many who possessed a taste for such productions, though not unfrequently men of various grades paid a visit to him who were not privileged to enjoy his conversation, as his work very often took him from home. On one such occasion two gentlemen alighted from a machine, and asked to be allowed a few minutes in his garden and museum. This was readily granted, Mrs Wilson being frequently called upon to give such opportunities. No special notice was taken of the two strangers by her, but after their departure a paper was found containing the following :—"We have to-day, when on a visit to Carlops, been permitted to visit the cottage and garden of Mr Charles Wilson, and having been previously informed of the many specimens of artistic skill, the productions of his own head and hands, we were consequently the less surprised, though not the less gratified, when we found ourselves in the midst of them. One thought which struck us very forcibly was this, that it was a great pity such decided genius should be allowed to remain in such a quiet though romantic village among the everlasting hills. How very different the remuneration it would bring, and how very different the opportunities presented for the development of such powers were such a man to be transplanted to a populous centre! We have on this occasion been deprived of the opportunity of enjoying conversation with one who proves his superiority in a manner which compels us to expect in such a man mental talents of a high order, unless it can be the case—which we cannot readily believe—that artistic skill can exist without such congenial companionship.

> 'Full many a gem of purest ray serene,
> The deep unfathomed caves of ocean bear;
> Full many a flower is born to blush unseen,
> And waste its sweetness on the desert air.'"

Mr Wilson, however, never yielded to any influence brought to bear on him with regard to leaving the district, but quietly plodded on, believing that man's true happiness consisted not altogether in the abundance of the things he possessed. What was very gratifying to him was the thought that his acquirements were not altogether misunderstood by those among whom he dwelt. On the contrary, in 1824, the dwellers in the district, sensible of his deservings, presented a lengthy memorial to the Secretary of the Highland Society, soliciting a consideration of his claim to one of their premiums. This memorial had the desired effect, and very shortly afterwards he was presented, through Mr James Maclean of Nine-Mile-Burn, with a medal bearing the following inscription:—"Voted by the Highland Society of Scotland, to Charles Wilson, parish of West Linton, as a mark of approbation in respect to the cleanliness and neatness with which the cottage occupied by him has been kept.—1824." The medal is in the possession of his son, William Wilson, in Penicuik, a gentleman now in advanced years, but who, in his youth, frequently assisted his father in his tedious and laborious undertakings.

The memorial presented to the Highland Society on behalf of Mr Wilson stated that "the individual we have taken the freedom to recommend resides in the village of Carlops—a village not only famed for its picturesque and truly romantic beauty, but for its being the scene which gave birth to our far-famed national comedy of 'The Gentle Shepherd.' The village is about fourteen miles from Edinburgh, the property of Robert Brown, Esq. of Newhall, advocate, and amidst the romantic peculiarities which distinguish it and which make it the resort of many visitors, the dwelling-house of Charles Wilson is not least conspicuous. Since the formation of this elegant little village his house has always been a model of neatness and cleanliness, and has been pointed out as such by every passing stranger. Possessing a genius superior to his situation in life, his little room may well be called a museum of natural and agricultural curiosities. The display of his genius has not stopped here, for he has erected with his own hands—although unlearned in the trade—in his little garden, a stone Temple of Gothic architecture which would compare with many of the famed productions of ancient or modern Athens.   Travellers who have seen it declare it to be the finest production of the kind in any village in the United Kingdom.   When once it is finished in the inside, it is our intention at some future period to present your Society with a drawing of it, along with a plan of his garden—a similar pattern of neatness. Sensible of the neglect to which genius in humble life is not unfrequently subjected, we feel we cannot make a better appeal to the consideration of a society of noblemen and gentlemen associated for the express purpose of encouraging by their illustrious patronage all that is ingenious in the mental capacity or distinguished in the active industry of Caledonia's sons, than in the feeling and warm-hearted effusion of a very distinguished member of your Society on visiting the late abode of a genius who, when living occupied a similar rank in humble life to the individual we have recommended to your consideration." The memorial concludes with the effusion alluded to, and which refers to a visit paid to the cottage at Gairney Bridge, near Kinross, where Michael Bruce the poet resided.

ROBERT SCOTT OF WOBURN.

WE have in these papers been speaking exclusively of persons who were either natives of or had a prolonged connection with the Carlops district.   There were other parties whose connection with the district was more transient, but who nevertheless figured conspicuously in local events.   Notable amongst these was one who came from Dryfesdale, and who in his humble position exhibited much of the chivalry of the genuine border man.   Robert Scott, farmer of Woburn, a small holding on Newhall estate, was a cousin of Sir Walter Scott, a relationship of which he was justly proud; and in recognition of which he called one of his sons by his name.   The name of Robert Scott was frequently before the public, sometimes as a composer of satire in verse, but oftener on account of his suspected exploits in smuggling; and the deft and skilful manner in

which he evaded the officers of the excise, in the words of
Burns, "set the world a' in a roar o' laughin' at them."

The last of these recorded of him was a capture at his
own dwelling at Woburn. The two gentlemen who were
successful had a machine which they left on the Edinburgh
road, his house being three hundred yards distant. Robert
Scott agreed at once to go with them, but on their way up,
and at a part of the road opposite a marshy and almost
impassable spot, he said to them, "Now I have treated
you as gentlemen, you will allow me a few seconds to
adjust my shoes." To this they frankly agreed; in an
instant, the tall and supple farmer of Woburn sprang over
the fence, and looking back on them with an air of defiance
said, "Now, gentlemen, in the words of my own illustrious
cousin, 'They'll hae fleet steeds that follow.'" It was
nearing the close of a dark November day, pursuit was
deemed alike hopeless and impracticable, and Scott vanished
from the sight of the crestfallen officers, who rather ruefully
regarded the escape of the smuggler, who had again proved
more than a match for them.

A RUN TO THE BIRTH-PLACE OF BURNS.

IT was in the fulfilment of a long cherished hope, that I found myself, on a bright July morning, on the way to the "Toon o' Ayr," Burns' Cottage, and Alloway's auld haunted Kirk. My companions were few and well chosen; the one, my first-born, a young man set free for a few days from the office and the desk; the other an old friend, a keen musician, and one who intelligently cherished an enthusiastic admiration of the sentiment, the patriotism, and the general beauty by which the writings of Robert Burns are characterised. Finding ourselves at Carstairs at an early hour, the question came to be—"Shall we go by Glasgow, or shall we choose the shorter route by Muirkirk?"—"The latter by all means," replied my friend. "The smoke, the bustle, the noise, and the excitement of the western metropolis can present but little attraction on a day when we expect for an hour to

'Linger by the Doon's low trees, or
Wander by the wood-crowned Ayr.'"

"Well," I replied, "by adopting the latter we may have our Covenanting proclivities revived by a glimpse of Aird's Moss, where Richard Cameron and a number of his followers fell in the memorable encounter which took place there in 1686, and where, in the words of the beautiful ballad which has doubtless deepened and intensified the interest taken in this bleak and lonely scene,

'Cameron's sword and his Bible are seen
Engrav'd on the stane where the heather grows green.'"

Passing from Lanark to Douglas the scenery is wonderfully diversified and interesting, but after passing the latter place it becomes bleak almost beyond description. Its monotony is now and again broken up by the appearance of a smoky, and frequently a smokeless chimney, telling the traveller of successful and unsuccessful experiments and enterprise into which men and companies have embarked.

Aird's Moss, as seen from the windows of a railway carriage, is an extensive, bleak, and apparently marshy tract of country; and a white pointed stone guides the eye to the place where lies the monument which we have already referred to in the words of Hyslop's ballad.

Arriving at the stations of Cumnock, Mauchline, and Auchinleck, we were now in classic ground, in the midst of scenes and places with whose names we were warmly interested, and which had been familiar to us as household words since our earliest years. In a very short time we found ourselves emerging from the elegant station bearing the honoured name of Ayr. "How late this train is," said my friend, "eleven o'clock."—"Yes," said I, hearing it chiming from a clock and tower in a conspicuous part of the town, "and I presume 'Wallace Tower has sworn the news is true.'" We had to leave by three o'clock, and it was now ours to make the best of the brief and bright hours of that July day. We set out to have a survey of the new and auld brigs, the old church of Ayr, and the churchyard, which of itself is sufficiently interesting to occupy an after-noon for any person with a taste for the historic and antique. It was Burns and Burns only, however, and we took our way out the beautiful road which, in his immortal poem of "Tam o' Shanter," he contrived to invest with such an endless variety of horrors. For one mile at least it is lined with neat and elegant villas with names betokening the tastes and preferences of the parties who have chosen such a spot as a desirable residence. After a walk of forty minutes we were standing within the precincts of the small churchyard of Alloway. The church presented almost exactly the appearance we had often cherished in our own mind regarding it, the only difference being that it was considerably smaller than we had imagined. The bell, which was wont for a long period to awaken the echoes of Doonside, but which has hung silent for a century, still remains in the antique belfry; the walls remain entire, and the whole is not without tangible and pleasant proof that the interesting ruin is valued as an interesting relic, representing one of the most masterly productions of the great master of the Scottish lyre. We were deeply interested while gazing in at one of the side windows to take a close and minute view of the walls where

"Coffins stood round like open presses," and in doing so we observed that the interior is now broken up by a mid wall or partition; the division furthest from the entrance being occupied as a burial-place by a family of eminence, while the division nearer the road is apparently used as a place for preserving implements of burial, such as we have seen in old ruined churches elsewhere. Our interest in the edifice, however, came to its climax when we surveyed the double lancet window in the end wall whose gable is surmounted by the belfry, and reached by a gently rising ground, such as we have heard our seniors speak of as a "Herst." At this window, which we could fancy a proper height from the ground to be looked in at on horseback, Tam reached the zenith of his excitement, as the poem does the culmination of its humour, when he roared out, "Weel done, cutty sark, and in an instant a' was dark." On the rising ground alluded to we found the flat tombstone to the poet's father, William Burns, as also one to another member of the family, both giving proof of careful preservation. In strolling through the churchyard, we passed and repassed group after group of young and old of both sexes, eagerly examining, as we were doing, every object of interest. They were engaged in conversation, and evidently had as little time at their disposal as we had at ours, yet were making the best of the passing moments in conveying to their note books and memories a durable impression of the scenes before them. My friend was anxious to carry away with him some small relic of the spot, but we need scarcely say that this being such a very common feeling among parties visiting the scenes we speak of, restrictions have been laid down, and precautions used, so that such is quite impracticable if not altogether impossible.

We now took a turn to the banks of Doon, choosing at the same time the old and more uneven and abrupt road where "Tam," pursued by the legion, hastened to "mak' the keystane o' the brig" It is quite in the style of the oldest bridges with which we are familiar, high in the centre and very narrow, and standing there we can see the new bridge, by which latter the road has been straightened and improved. The Doon is "bonnie" in the strictest sense in which that word, so thoroughly Scottish, can be applied. It is a quiet running stream, with a soft ripple, reminding us of the words of one of Burns' most ardent admirers, the Rev. Hamilton Paul.

> "Here Doon in slow meanders glides along,
> 'Mid banks that bloom for ever in his song."

Its course for a considerable distance is through a deep valley, embowered among copious foliage, with every feature to render it attractive to the artist or the poet.

The brevity of our time prevented us from inspecting the interior of his monument, which occupies a most commanding site on the rising ground between the Doon and the elegant new Parish Church. Hastening to his Cottage, we there found ourselves in the centre of all that was interesting. The kitchen, that apartment in which the poet was born, undoubtedly retains much of its primitive appearance—the homely fire-place over which hangs the girdle, the venerable eight day clock, the old oak table on which are ingeniously carved one hundred initials, and the humble bed in which Burns was born. "Now," said I to my friend, "we can use the language of Halleck the American poet as he sings,

> 'I've stood beside the cottage bed
> Where that bard peasant first drew breath,
> A straw-thatched roof above his head,
> A straw-wrought couch beneath.
>
> And I have stood beside that pile,
> His monument, that tells to heaven
> The homage of earth's proudest isle,
> To that bard peasant given.'

We are standing on ground sacred to every intelligent Scotchman at home and abroad, where the greatest hearts, and most patriotic breasts of generations have felt it an honour to stand, and gazing on objects unsurpassed in interest to the honest sons and fair daughters of our native land. What an interest attaches itself to this humble apartment, were it in nothing more than the remembrance of the great and distinguished personages who have found pleasure, such as we now enjoy, when standing beneath this lowly roof. Again the words of Halleck are fresh in my memory, when he says,

‘ Pilgrims whose wandering feet have pressed
   The Switzer's snow, the Arab's sand,
Or trod the piled leaves of the west,
   My own green forest land.

Sages with wisdom's garland wreathed,
   Crown'd kings and mitred priests of power,
And warriors with their bright swords sheathed—
   The mightiest of the hour ;

And lowlier names whose humble home
   Is lit by fortune's dimmer star,
Are there, o'er wave and mountain come,
   From countries near and far.

All ask the cottage of his birth,
   Gaze on the scenes he lov'd and sung,
And gather feelings not of earth,
   His fields and streams among.’

What do think, then," said I to my friend, "of this humble
domicile ?"—"Oh, well," he replied, "everything here
reminds me of ‘The Cottar's Saturday nicht.’"—"I am
sure," said a gentleman who had overheard part of our
conversation, "it must be a ground of satisfaction to you,
that this interesting dwelling-place is no longer used as a
place for the sale of intoxicating drink."—"Most decidedly
so," I replied, "and how gratifying to see the continuous
coming and going of groups of young and old, of male and
female visitors here, at his monument, and in Alloway
Churchyard, sober and orderly, without the slightest
indication of intoxicating drinks having been used by them.
In my humble estimation the parties who were instrumental
in bringing about such a result have laid claim to a nation's
gratitude ; for among the thousand tributes of respect paid
to the memory of poor Burns, no more kindly work of
genuine and consistent admiration was ever contributed to
his memory than the abolition of this stigma."—"I am
happy to hear such sentiments expressed," he rejoined ;
"and do you not think it is a pity that Burns, when alive,
enjoyed so little of the honour now reaped upon his name ?
If he had lived now do you not think he would have met
with a different reception ?"—"Little doubt," I said, "with
the present more general intelligence and fuller liberty for
the expression of opinion, the circle of his admirers would

have been wider. But were another Burns to appear, charged with such a mission, and in as faithful and fearless a fulfilment of the same were to tear the rotten rags from hypocrisy and dissemblance, and wield his club in as unmerciful a manner against cant and pretence, there is still a class, and that not a small one, who would feel the wound inflicted very keenly. Jealousy and hatred would be cherished, and anathemas would be hurled at him with as much vehemence as they were at Burns, by the little narrow-minded men, cleric and lay, who looked upon him as a source of annoyance, a vulgar writer of doggerel, who dared to interfere with men holding high position, little dreaming that the keen cutting satires which they and their eccentricities had been the means of calling forth were to be the admiration of their countrymen centuries after their names had been decently consigned to oblivion. Or if they were in any degree rescued from such, it was simply because they had—fortunately or unfortunately—been brought into contact with Burns and had had a little notoriety annexed to their names when in his own words he

> Set the warld a' in a roar
> O' lauchin' at them."

After a glance at that part of the building used as a museum, and where are carefully preserved a variety of very interesting relics, and bidding our new friend good-bye, we hastened back to Ayr, and when taking a parting look of his cottage and the scenery surrounding, we called to mind the words of a humble "son of toil" regarding them—

> A sacred spot, the lowly cot,
>   Where first life's breath he drew,
> The vales and glens through which he strayed,
>   Are they not classic too?
>
> Yea, every stream of which he sung,
>   And every winding river,
> A "thing of beauty" hath become,
>   Ay, and "a joy for ever."

Our time permitted us to make only a brief call at the Tam o' Shanter Inn, where we were shown the chairs, supposed to be those in which the two heroes of the bowl sat, and on both of which are plates bearing inscriptions in confirmation of the idea. Whether this is actually the house in which their convivialities took place we are not prepared to discuss, nor called upon to decide. We will venture to say, however, that appearances are much in its favour. It presents the snug, cosy, and comfortable appearance of the wayside inns, more common thirty or forty years ago than now; and we can easily understand how a few kindly and genial spirits could, seated beside an ingle bleezin' finely, and with the use of the ale which was aye growin' better, forget the storm that was ragin' without, and the lang and eerie road to be travelled before hame was reached.

By three o'clock we were pursuing our journey homeward, and after passing the station of Old Cumnock, we found ourselves among the wilds of Glenbuck and Muirkirk, enjoying a second glance at Aird's Moss. With the beautiful sunset was closed one of those days which must remain fresh in our memory; for though we have often with much interest wandered o'er the weary moorland to visit the plain, rude stone which told of the resting-place of one who had died in defence of the Word of God and Scotland's Covenanted work of Reformation, or sought the lonely battlefield whose name is inseparable from a Wallace or a Bruce, or the venerable ecclesiastical ruin which remained as a monument of centuries long gone by, yet, on none of these occasions were we under the influence of such pleasurable feelings as those experienced when visiting the banks o' Doon, Alloway Kirk, and the Cottage wherein Burns was born.